POWER CODERS

THE SECRET OF THE FIVE BUGS

C.R. McKAY

ILLUSTRATED BY JOEL GENNARI

PowerKiDS
press.

New York

Published in 2019 by The Rosen Publishing Group, Inc.
29 East 21st Street, New York, NY 10010

First Edition

Illustrator: Joel Gennari
Interior Layout: Tanya Dellaccio
Managing Editor: Nathalie Beullens-Maoui
Editorial Director: Greg Roza

Cataloging-in-Publication Data

Names: McKay, C.R.
Title: The secret of the five bugs / C.R. McKay.
Description: New York : PowerKids Press, 2019. | Series: Power coders
Identifiers: LCCN ISBN 9781538340141 (pbk.) | ISBN 9781538340134 (library bound) | ISBN 9781538340158 (6 pack)
Subjects: LCSH: Computer programming–Juvenile fiction. | Computer science–Juvenile fiction. | Insects–Juvenile fiction.
Classification: LCC PZ7.1.M43543 Se 2019 | DDC [E]–dc23

Manufactured in the United States of America

CPSIA Compliance Information: Batch CS18PK: For Further Information contact Rosen Publishing, New York, New York at 1-800-237-9932

CONTENTS

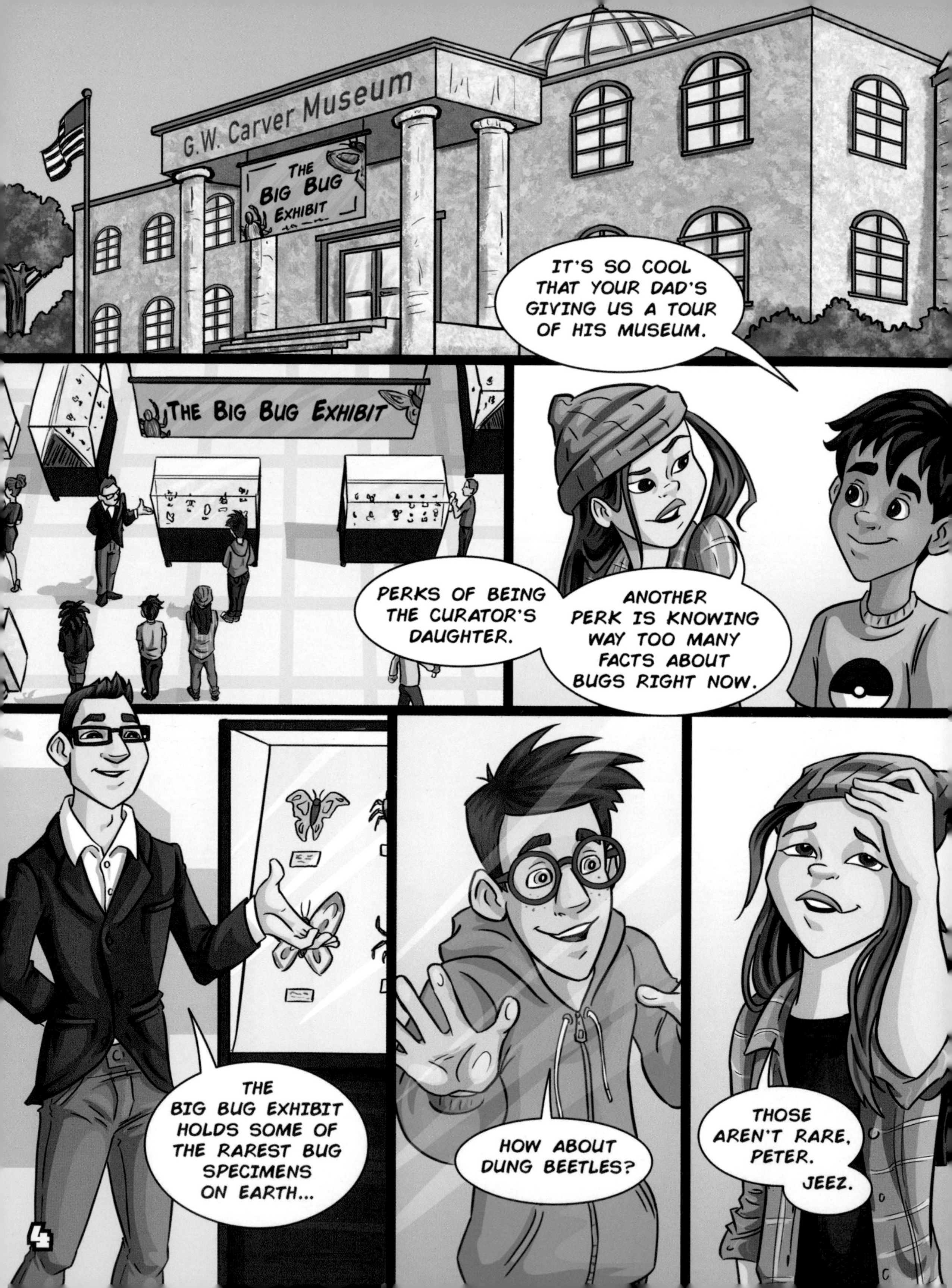
G.W. Carver Museum
THE BIG BUG EXHIBIT
IT'S SO COOL THAT YOUR DAD'S GIVING US A TOUR OF HIS MUSEUM.
THE BIG BUG EXHIBIT
PERKS OF BEING THE CURATOR'S DAUGHTER.
ANOTHER PERK IS KNOWING WAY TOO MANY FACTS ABOUT BUGS RIGHT NOW.
THE BIG BUG EXHIBIT HOLDS SOME OF THE RAREST BUG SPECIMENS ON EARTH...
HOW ABOUT DUNG BEETLES?
THOSE AREN'T RARE, PETER.
JEEZ.

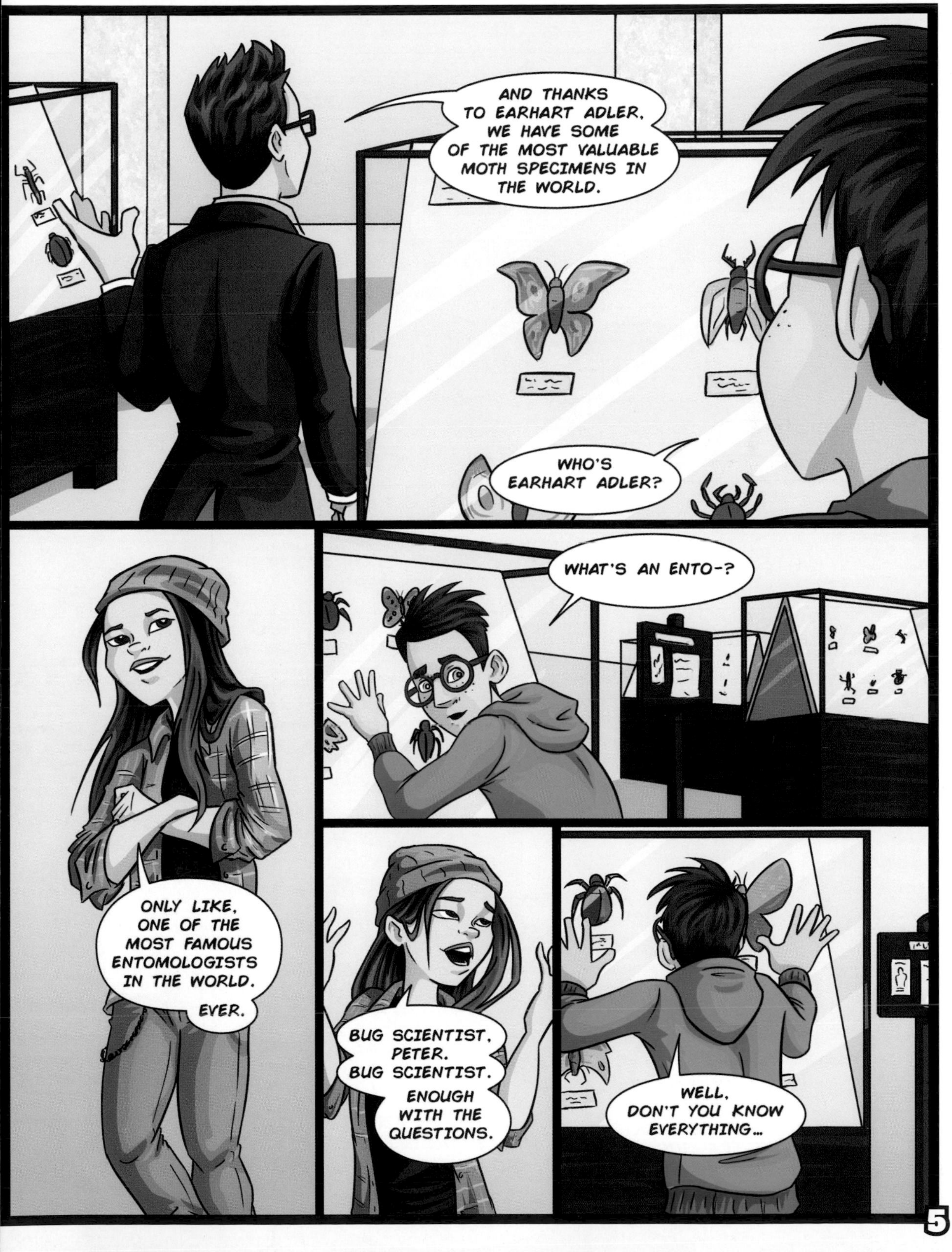
AND THANKS TO EARHART ADLER, WE HAVE SOME OF THE MOST VALUABLE MOTH SPECIMENS IN THE WORLD.
WHO'S EARHART ADLER?
ONLY LIKE, ONE OF THE MOST FAMOUS ENTOMOLOGISTS IN THE WORLD.
EVER.
WHAT'S AN ENTO-?
BUG SCIENTIST, PETER. BUG SCIENTIST.
ENOUGH WITH THE QUESTIONS.
WELL, DON'T YOU KNOW EVERYTHING...

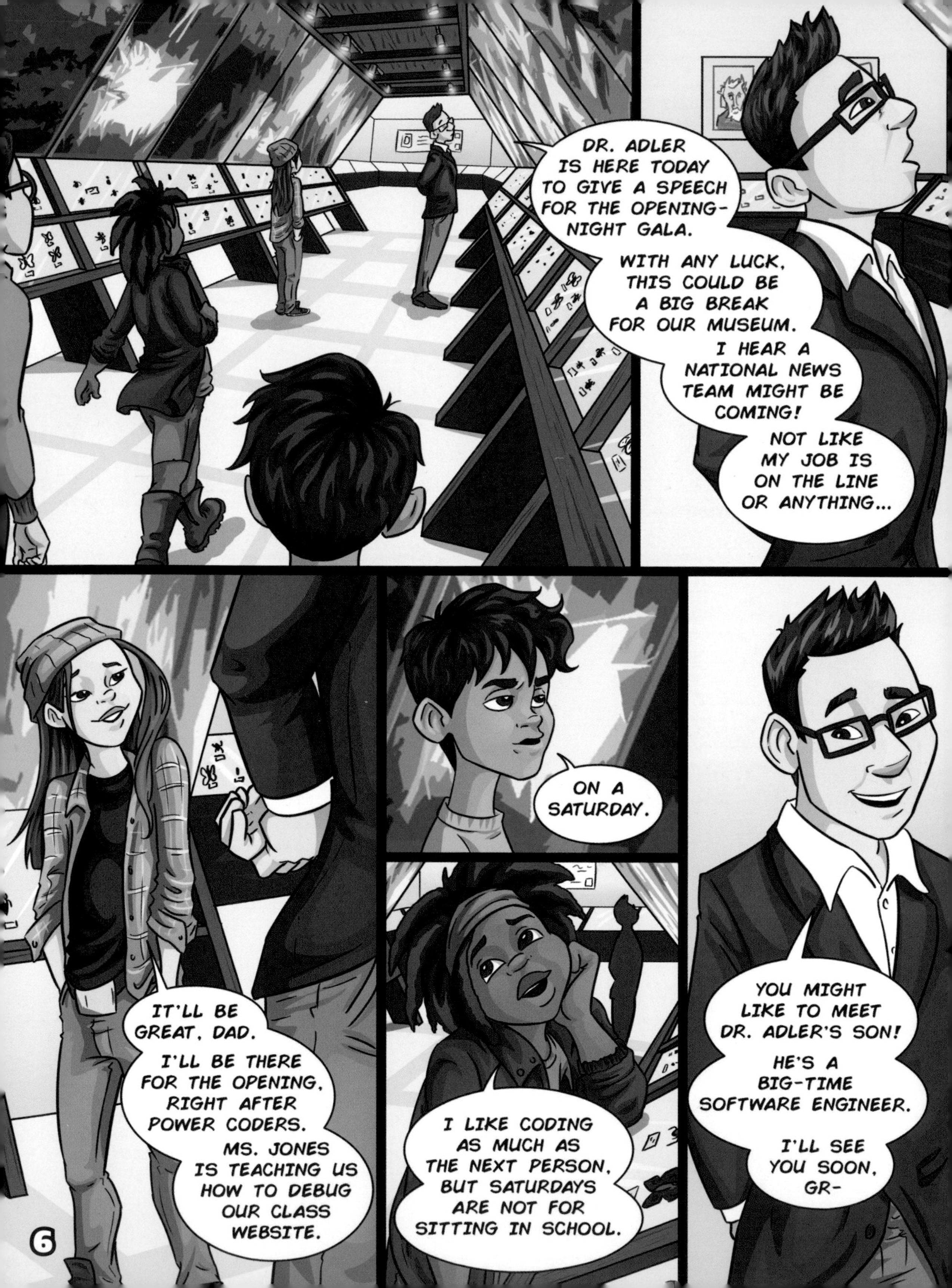
DR. ADLER IS HERE TODAY TO GIVE A SPEECH FOR THE OPENING-NIGHT GALA.
WITH ANY LUCK, THIS COULD BE A BIG BREAK FOR OUR MUSEUM.
I HEAR A NATIONAL NEWS TEAM MIGHT BE COMING!
NOT LIKE MY JOB IS ON THE LINE OR ANYTHING...
IT'LL BE GREAT, DAD.
I'LL BE THERE FOR THE OPENING, RIGHT AFTER POWER CODERS.
MS. JONES IS TEACHING US HOW TO DEBUG OUR CLASS WEBSITE.
ON A SATURDAY.
I LIKE CODING AS MUCH AS THE NEXT PERSON, BUT SATURDAYS ARE NOT FOR SITTING IN SCHOOL.
YOU MIGHT LIKE TO MEET DR. ADLER'S SON!
HE'S A BIG-TIME SOFTWARE ENGINEER.
I'LL SEE YOU SOON, GR-

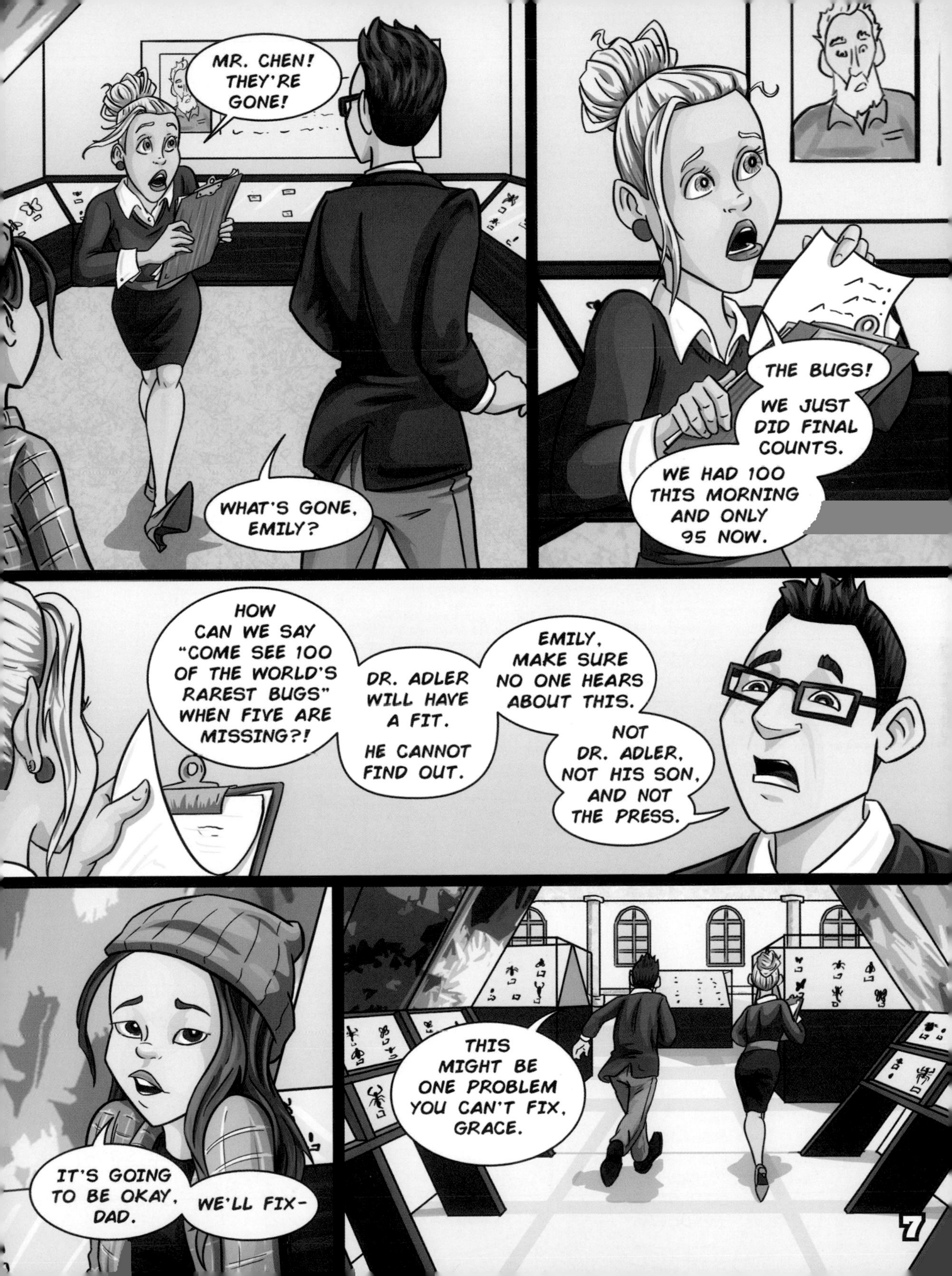
MR. CHEN! THEY'RE GONE!
WHAT'S GONE, EMILY?
THE BUGS!
WE JUST DID FINAL COUNTS.
WE HAD 100 THIS MORNING AND ONLY 95 NOW.
HOW CAN WE SAY "COME SEE 100 OF THE WORLD'S RAREST BUGS" WHEN FIVE ARE MISSING?!
DR. ADLER WILL HAVE A FIT.
HE CANNOT FIND OUT.
EMILY, MAKE SURE NO ONE HEARS ABOUT THIS.
NOT DR. ADLER, NOT HIS SON, AND NOT THE PRESS.
IT'S GOING TO BE OKAY, DAD.
WE'LL FIX-
THIS MIGHT BE ONE PROBLEM YOU CAN'T FIX, GRACE.

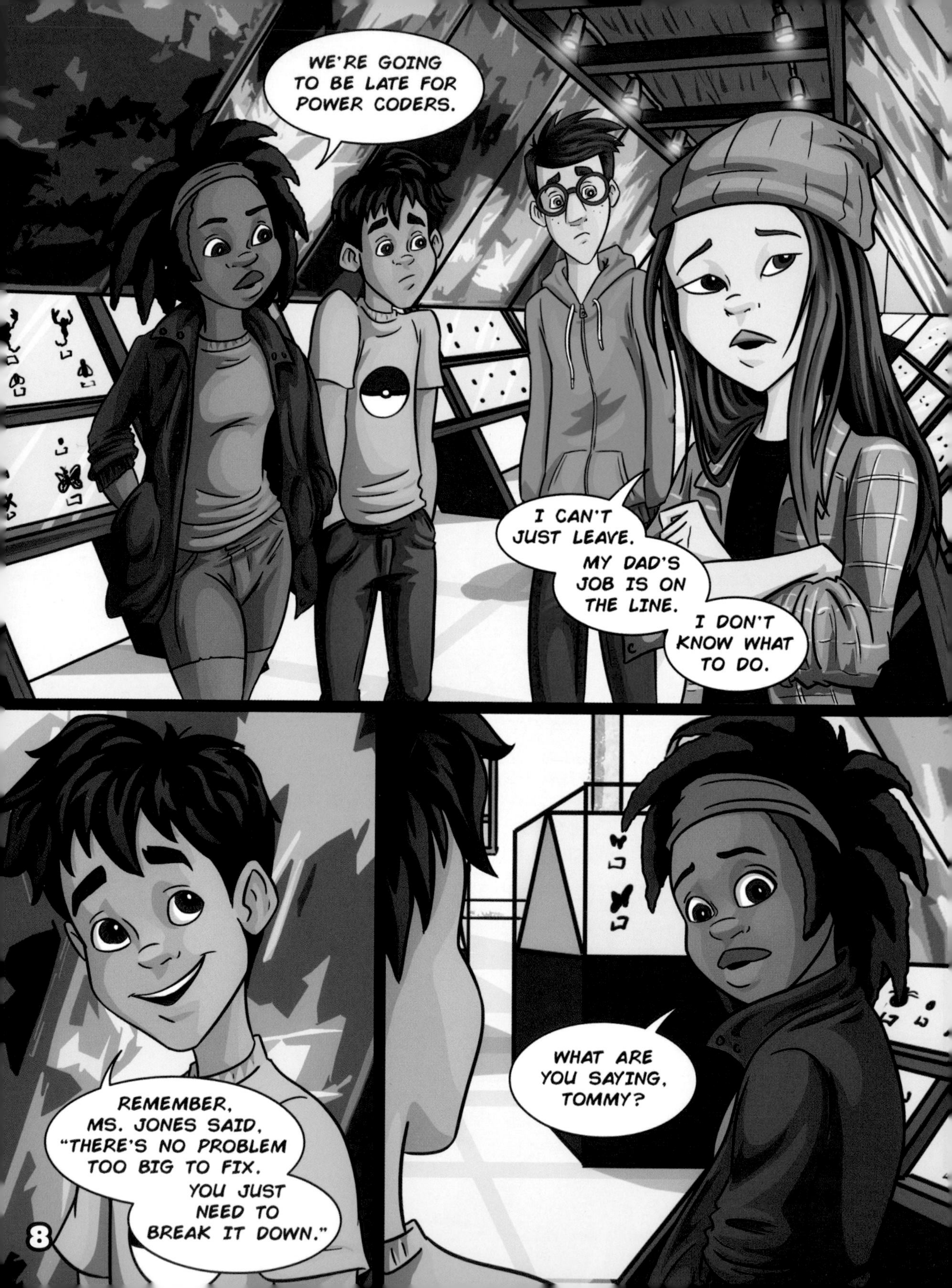
WE'RE GOING TO BE LATE FOR POWER CODERS.
I CAN'T JUST LEAVE.
MY DAD'S JOB IS ON THE LINE.
I DON'T KNOW WHAT TO DO.
REMEMBER, MS. JONES SAID, "THERE'S NO PROBLEM TOO BIG TO FIX.
YOU JUST NEED TO BREAK IT DOWN."
WHAT ARE YOU SAYING, TOMMY?

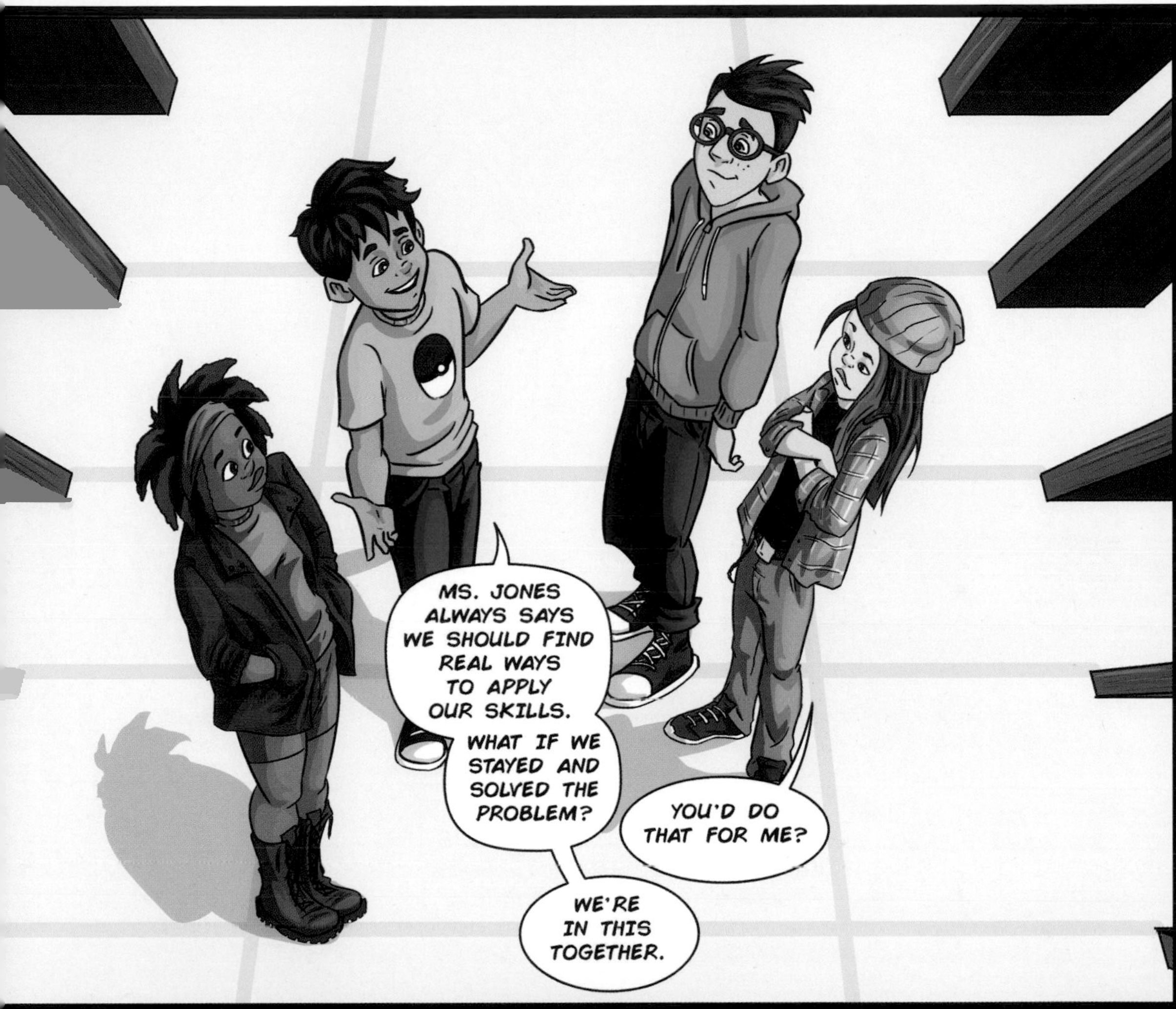
MS. JONES ALWAYS SAYS WE SHOULD FIND REAL WAYS TO APPLY OUR SKILLS.
WHAT IF WE STAYED AND SOLVED THE PROBLEM?
YOU'D DO THAT FOR ME?
WE'RE IN THIS TOGETHER.

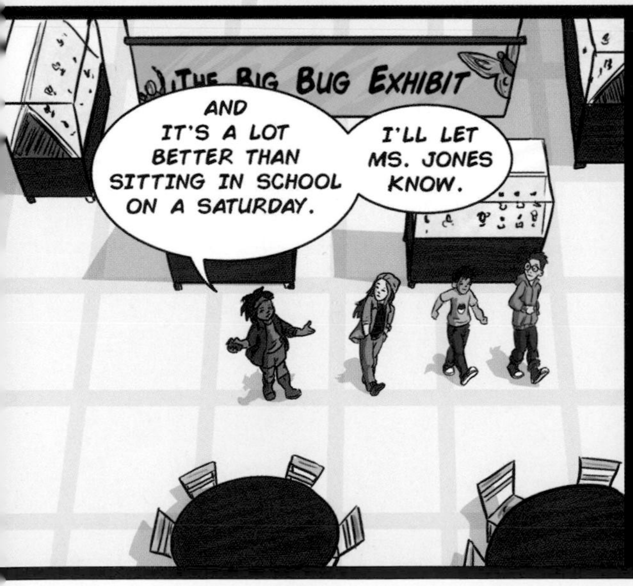
THE BIG BUG EXHIBIT
AND IT'S A LOT BETTER THAN SITTING IN SCHOOL ON A SATURDAY.
I'LL LET MS. JONES KNOW.

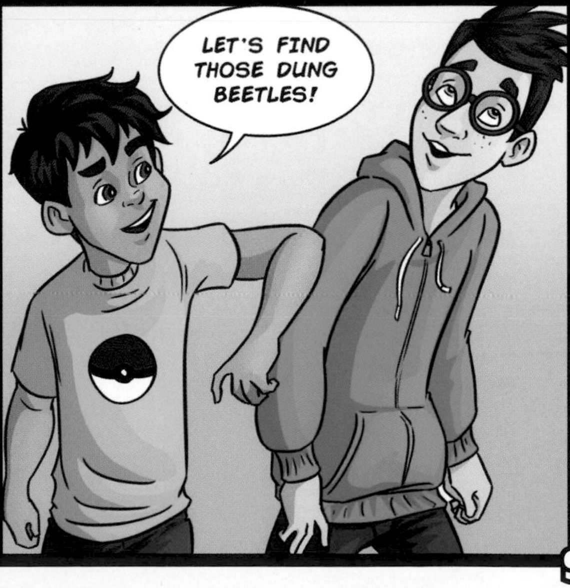
LET'S FIND THOSE DUNG BEETLES!

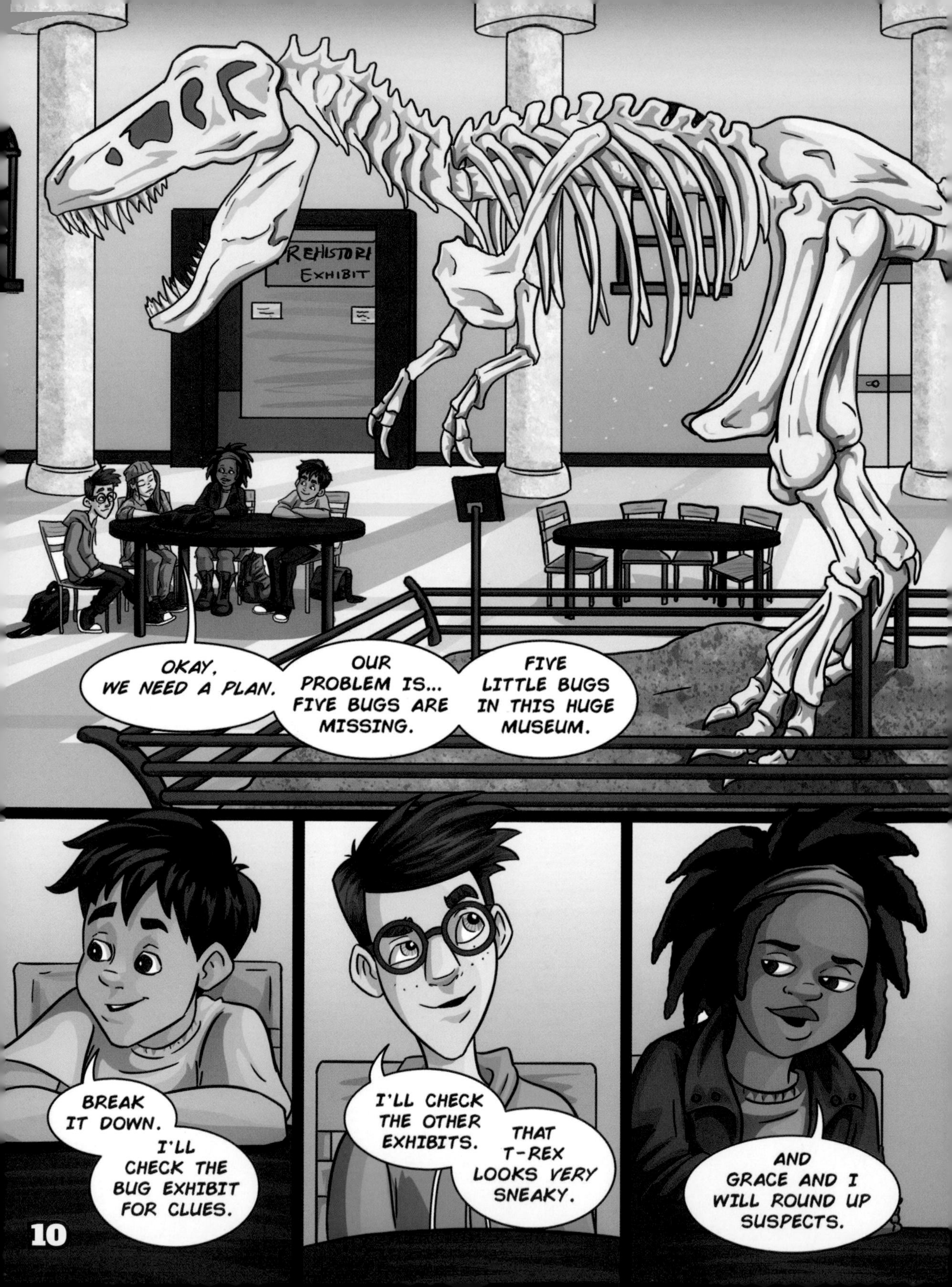
EXHIBIT
OKAY, WE NEED A PLAN.
OUR PROBLEM IS... FIVE BUGS ARE MISSING.
FIVE LITTLE BUGS IN THIS HUGE MUSEUM.
BREAK IT DOWN.
I'LL CHECK THE BUG EXHIBIT FOR CLUES.
I'LL CHECK THE OTHER EXHIBITS.
THAT T-REX LOOKS VERY SNEAKY.
AND GRACE AND I WILL ROUND UP SUSPECTS.

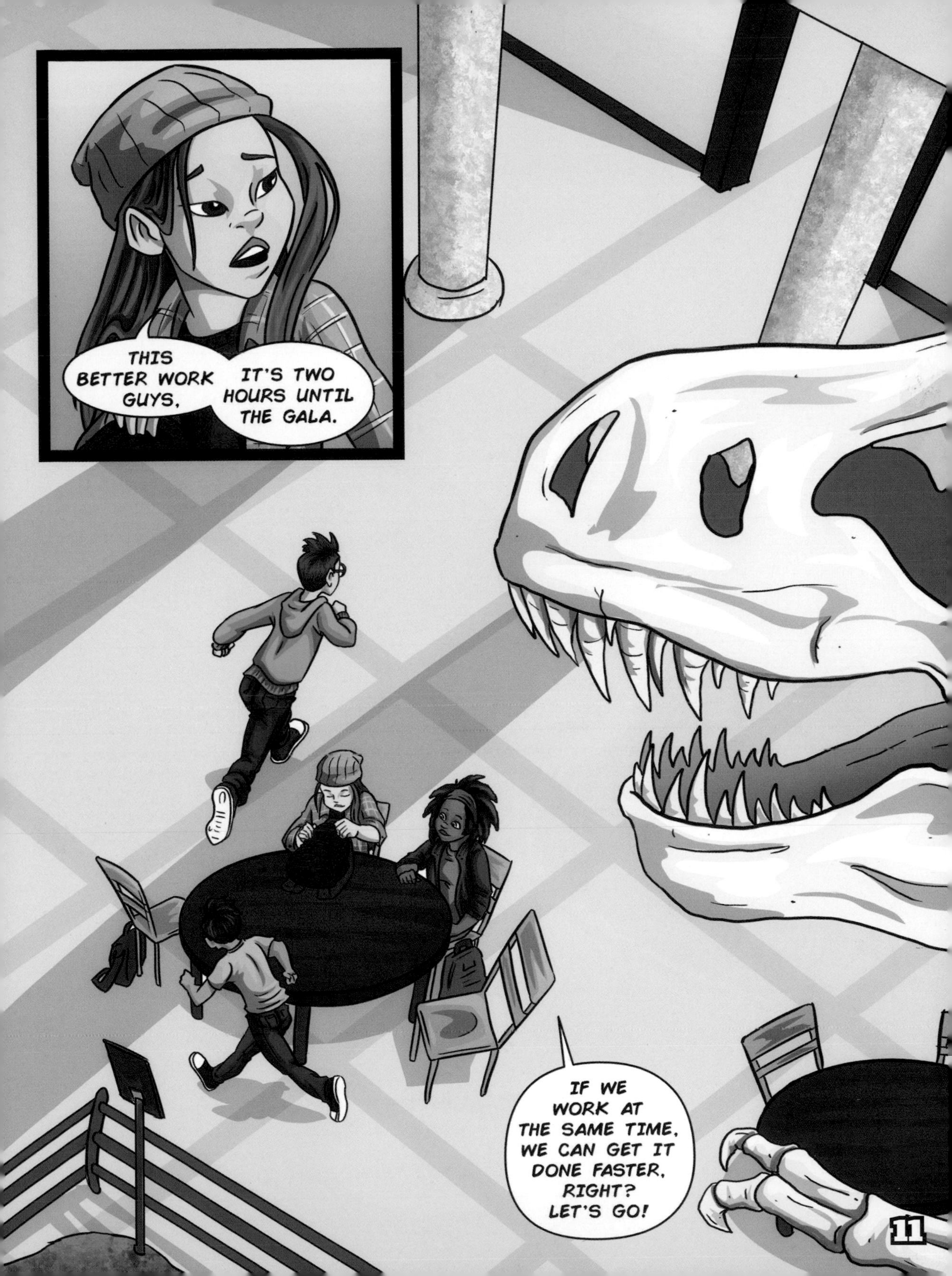
THIS BETTER WORK GUYS,
IT'S TWO HOURS UNTIL THE GALA.
IF WE WORK AT THE SAME TIME, WE CAN GET IT DONE FASTER, RIGHT? LET'S GO!

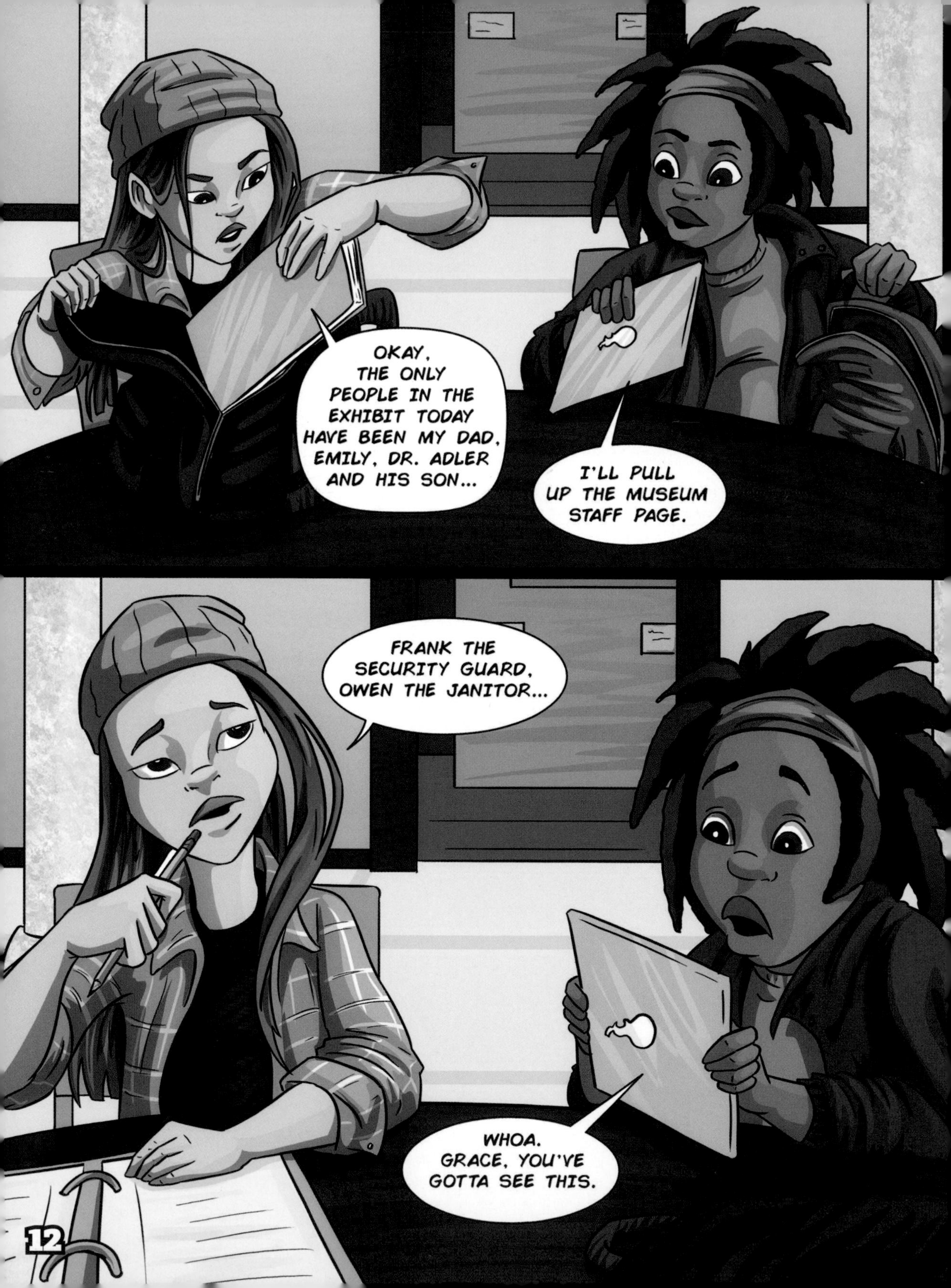
OKAY, THE ONLY PEOPLE IN THE EXHIBIT TODAY HAVE BEEN MY DAD, EMILY, DR. ADLER AND HIS SON...
I'LL PULL UP THE MUSEUM STAFF PAGE.
FRANK THE SECURITY GUARD, OWEN THE JANITOR...
WHOA. GRACE, YOU'VE GOTTA SEE THIS.

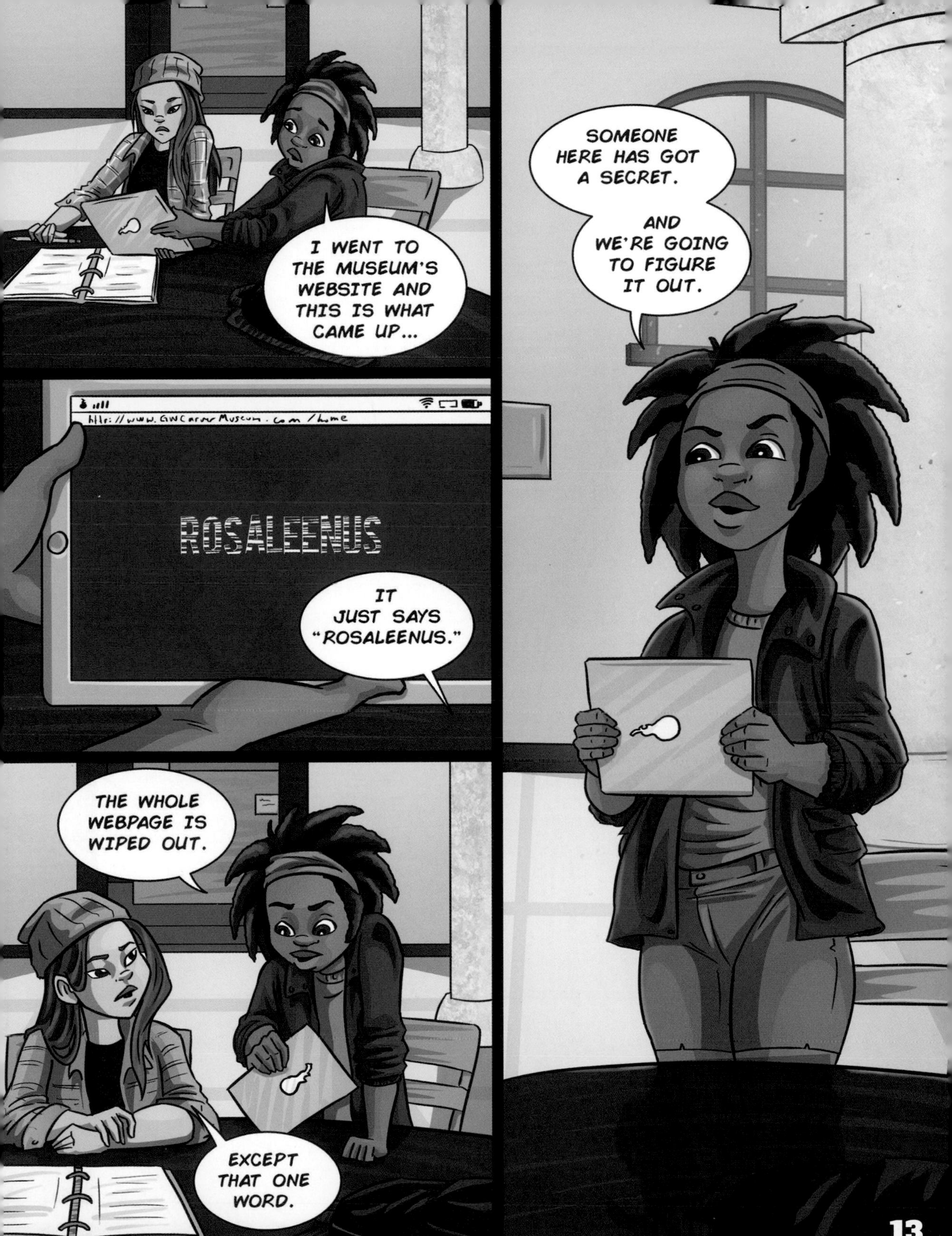
I WENT TO THE MUSEUM'S WEBSITE AND THIS IS WHAT CAME UP...
http://www.GWCarverMuseum.com/home
ROSALEENUS
IT JUST SAYS "ROSALEENUS."
THE WHOLE WEBPAGE IS WIPED OUT.
EXCEPT THAT ONE WORD.
SOMEONE HERE HAS GOT A SECRET.
AND WE'RE GOING TO FIGURE IT OUT.

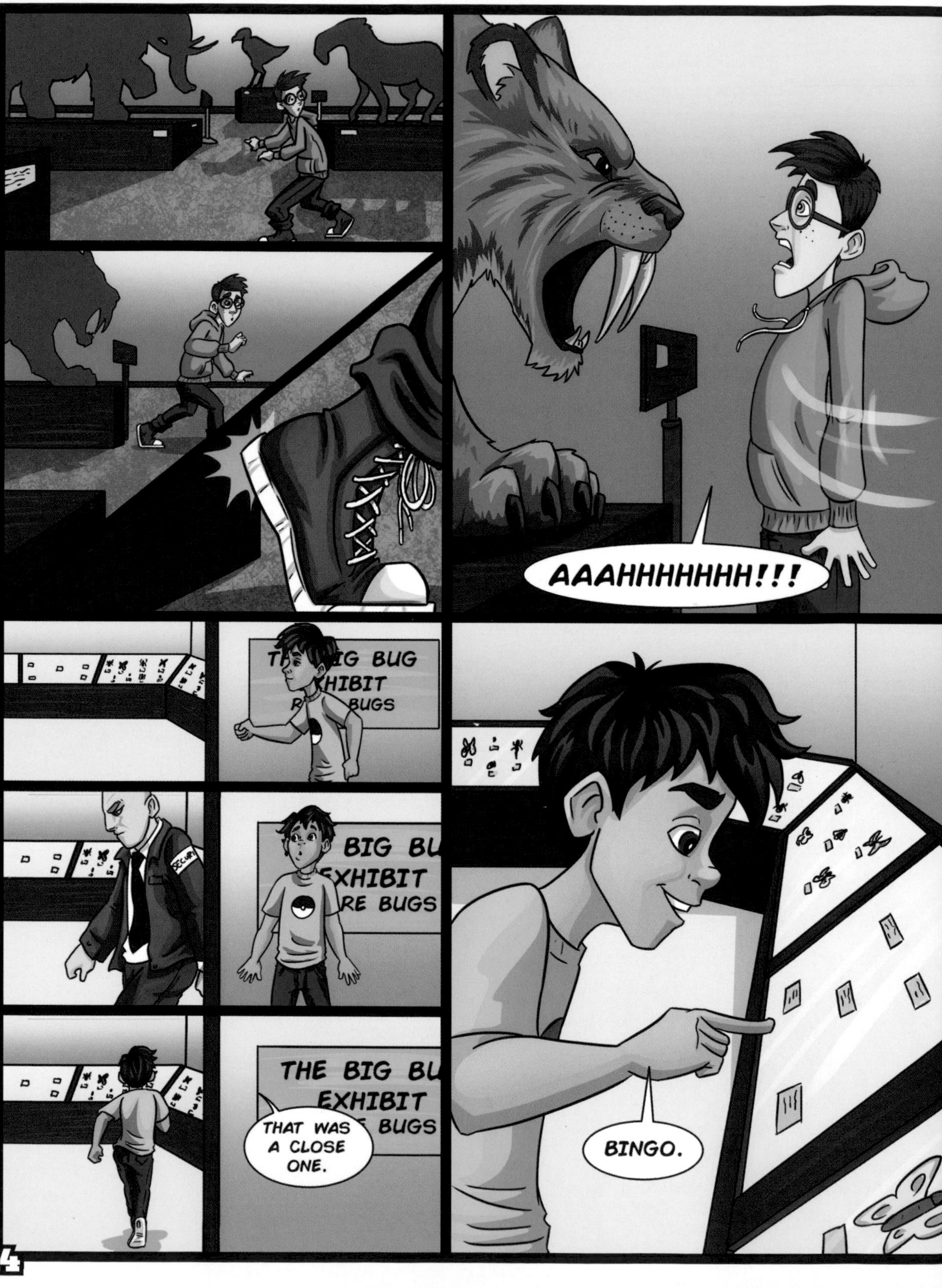
AAAHHHHHHH!!!
THAT WAS A CLOSE ONE.
BINGO.

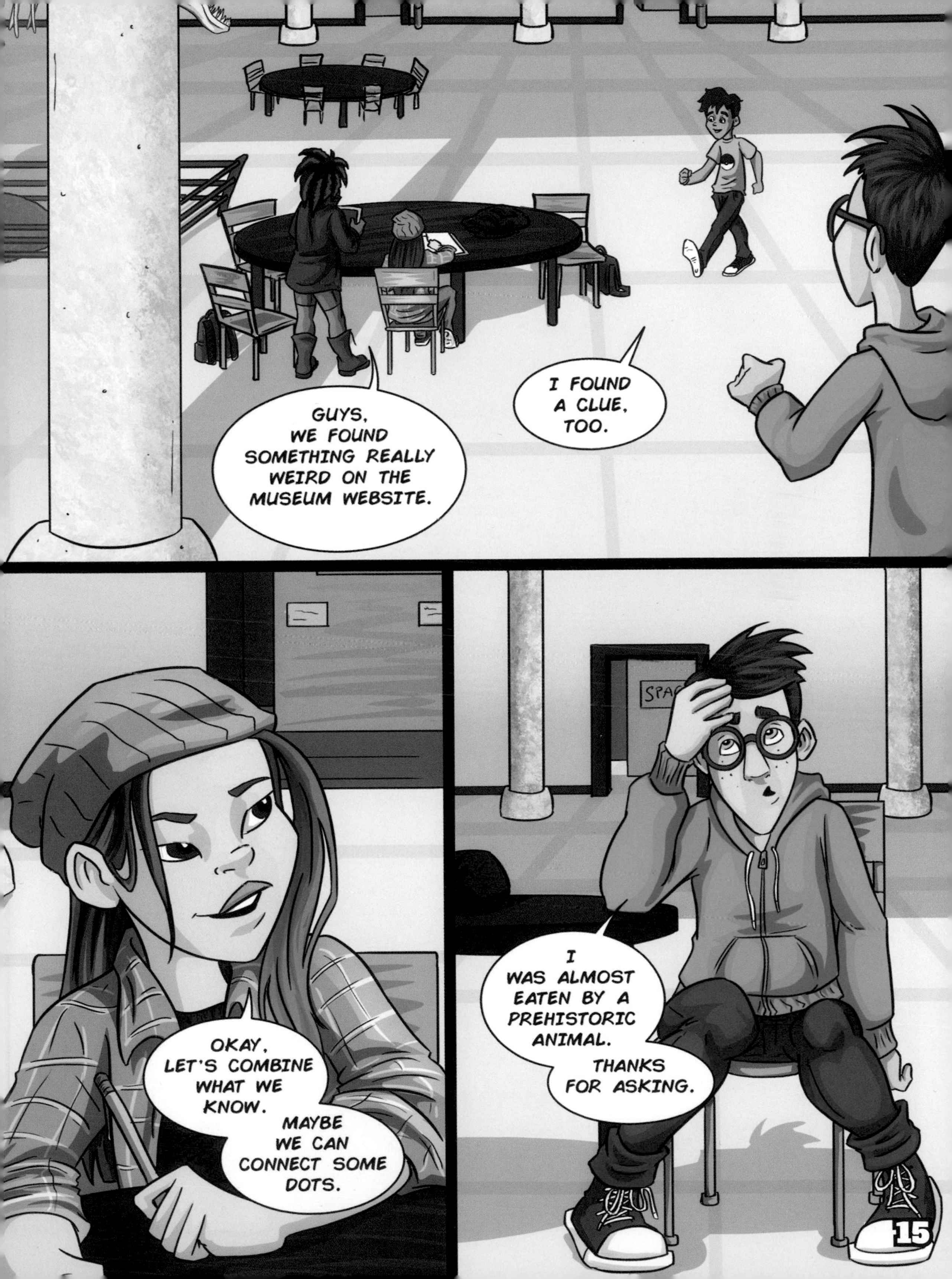
GUYS, WE FOUND SOMETHING REALLY WEIRD ON THE MUSEUM WEBSITE.
I FOUND A CLUE, TOO.
OKAY, LET'S COMBINE WHAT WE KNOW.
MAYBE WE CAN CONNECT SOME DOTS.
I WAS ALMOST EATEN BY A PREHISTORIC ANIMAL.
THANKS FOR ASKING.

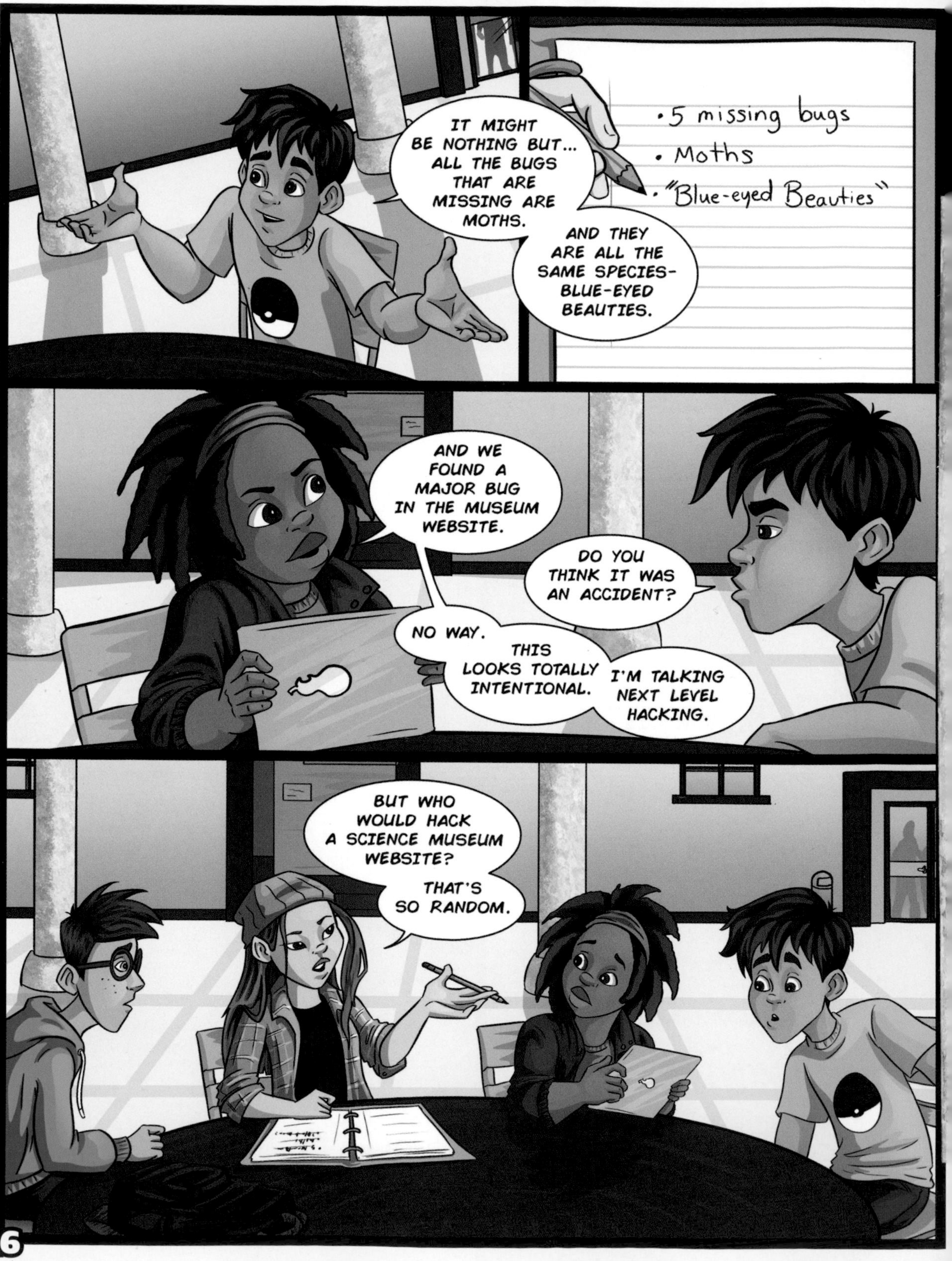
IT MIGHT BE NOTHING BUT... ALL THE BUGS THAT ARE MISSING ARE MOTHS.
AND THEY ARE ALL THE SAME SPECIES- BLUE-EYED BEAUTIES.
• 5 missing bugs
• Moths
• "Blue-eyed Beauties"
AND WE FOUND A MAJOR BUG IN THE MUSEUM WEBSITE.
DO YOU THINK IT WAS AN ACCIDENT?
NO WAY.
THIS LOOKS TOTALLY INTENTIONAL.
I'M TALKING NEXT LEVEL HACKING.
BUT WHO WOULD HACK A SCIENCE MUSEUM WEBSITE?
THAT'S SO RANDOM.

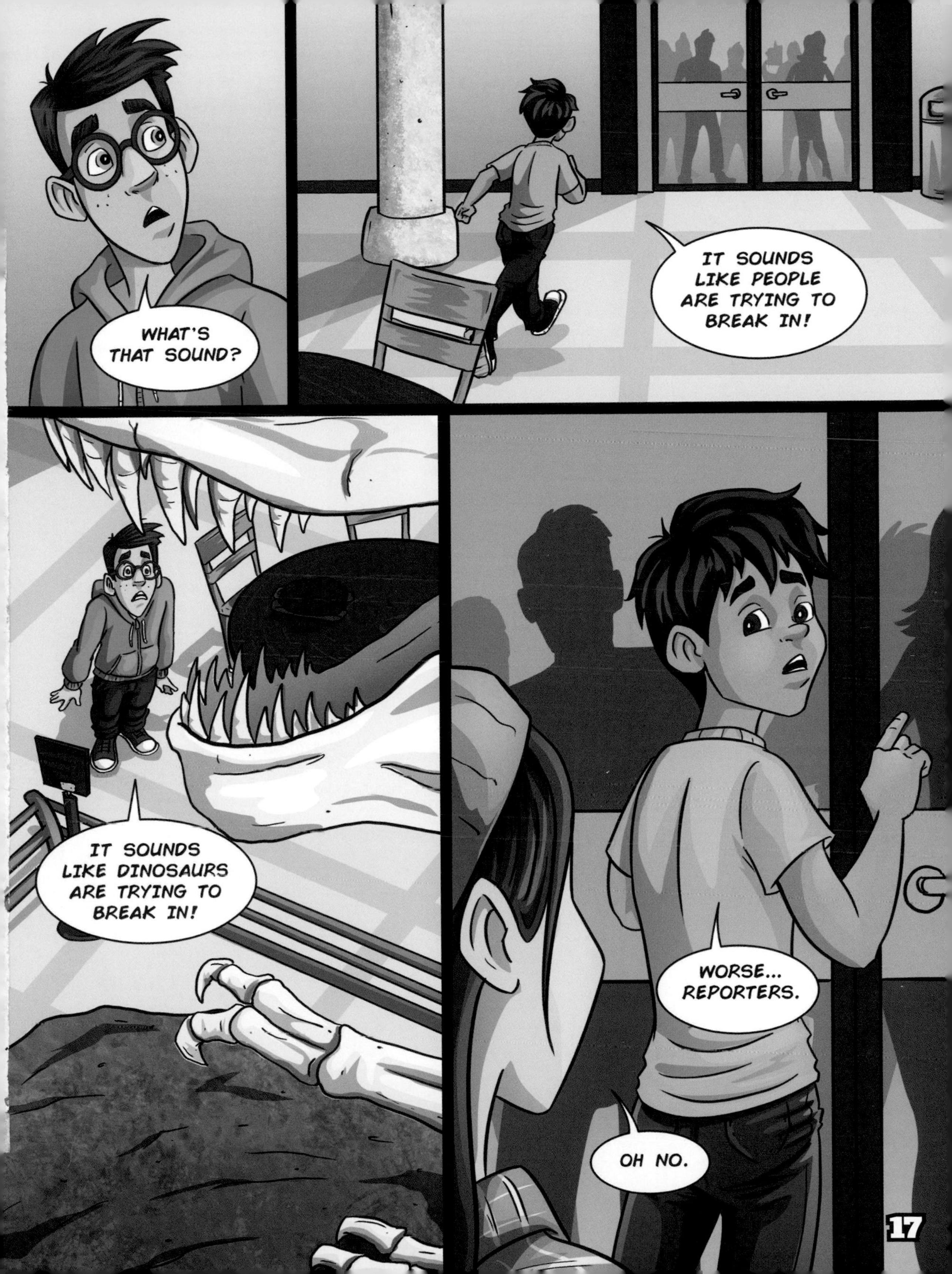
WHAT'S THAT SOUND?
IT SOUNDS LIKE PEOPLE ARE TRYING TO BREAK IN!
IT SOUNDS LIKE DINOSAURS ARE TRYING TO BREAK IN!
WORSE... REPORTERS.
OH NO.

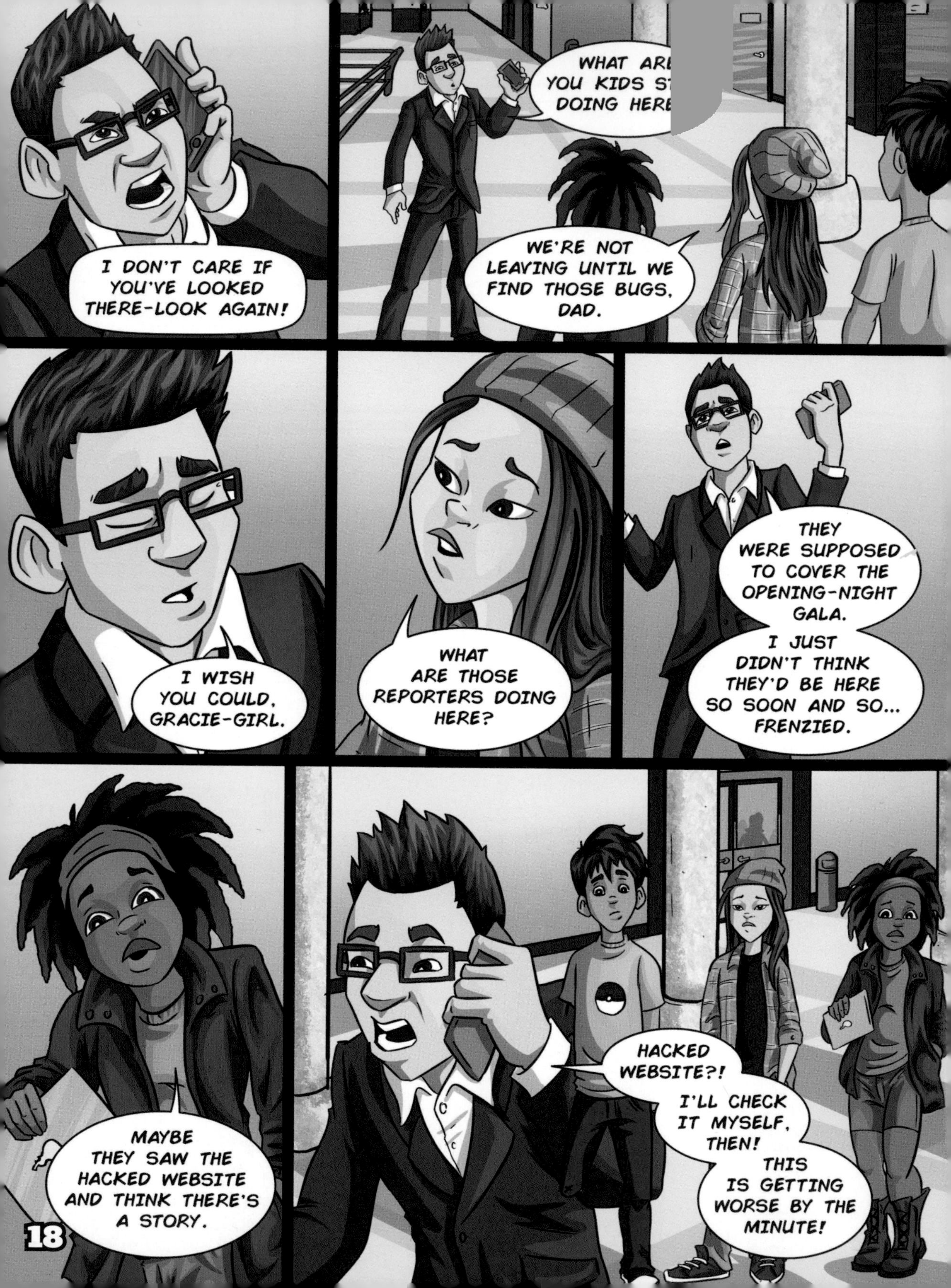
I DON'T CARE IF YOU'VE LOOKED THERE-LOOK AGAIN!
WHAT AR YOU KIDS ST DOING HERE
WE'RE NOT LEAVING UNTIL WE FIND THOSE BUGS, DAD.
I WISH YOU COULD, GRACIE-GIRL.
WHAT ARE THOSE REPORTERS DOING HERE?
THEY WERE SUPPOSED TO COVER THE OPENING-NIGHT GALA.
I JUST DIDN'T THINK THEY'D BE HERE SO SOON AND SO... FRENZIED.
MAYBE THEY SAW THE HACKED WEBSITE AND THINK THERE'S A STORY.
HACKED WEBSITE?!
I'LL CHECK IT MYSELF, THEN!
THIS IS GETTING WORSE BY THE MINUTE!

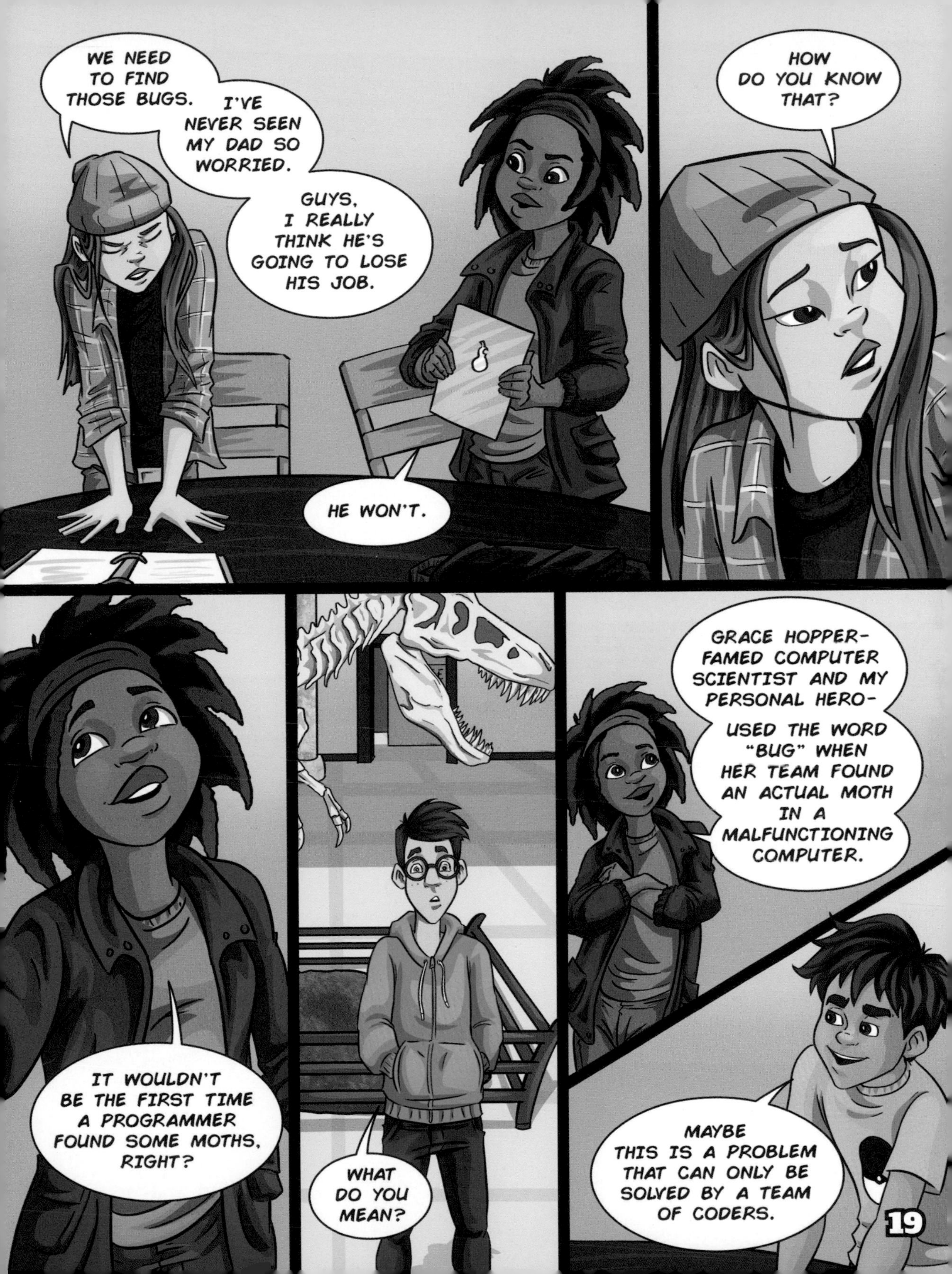
WE NEED TO FIND THOSE BUGS.
I'VE NEVER SEEN MY DAD SO WORRIED.
GUYS, I REALLY THINK HE'S GOING TO LOSE HIS JOB.
HE WON'T.
HOW DO YOU KNOW THAT?
IT WOULDN'T BE THE FIRST TIME A PROGRAMMER FOUND SOME MOTHS, RIGHT?
WHAT DO YOU MEAN?
GRACE HOPPER-FAMED COMPUTER SCIENTIST AND MY PERSONAL HERO-
USED THE WORD "BUG" WHEN HER TEAM FOUND AN ACTUAL MOTH IN A MALFUNCTIONING COMPUTER.
MAYBE THIS IS A PROBLEM THAT CAN ONLY BE SOLVED BY A TEAM OF CODERS.

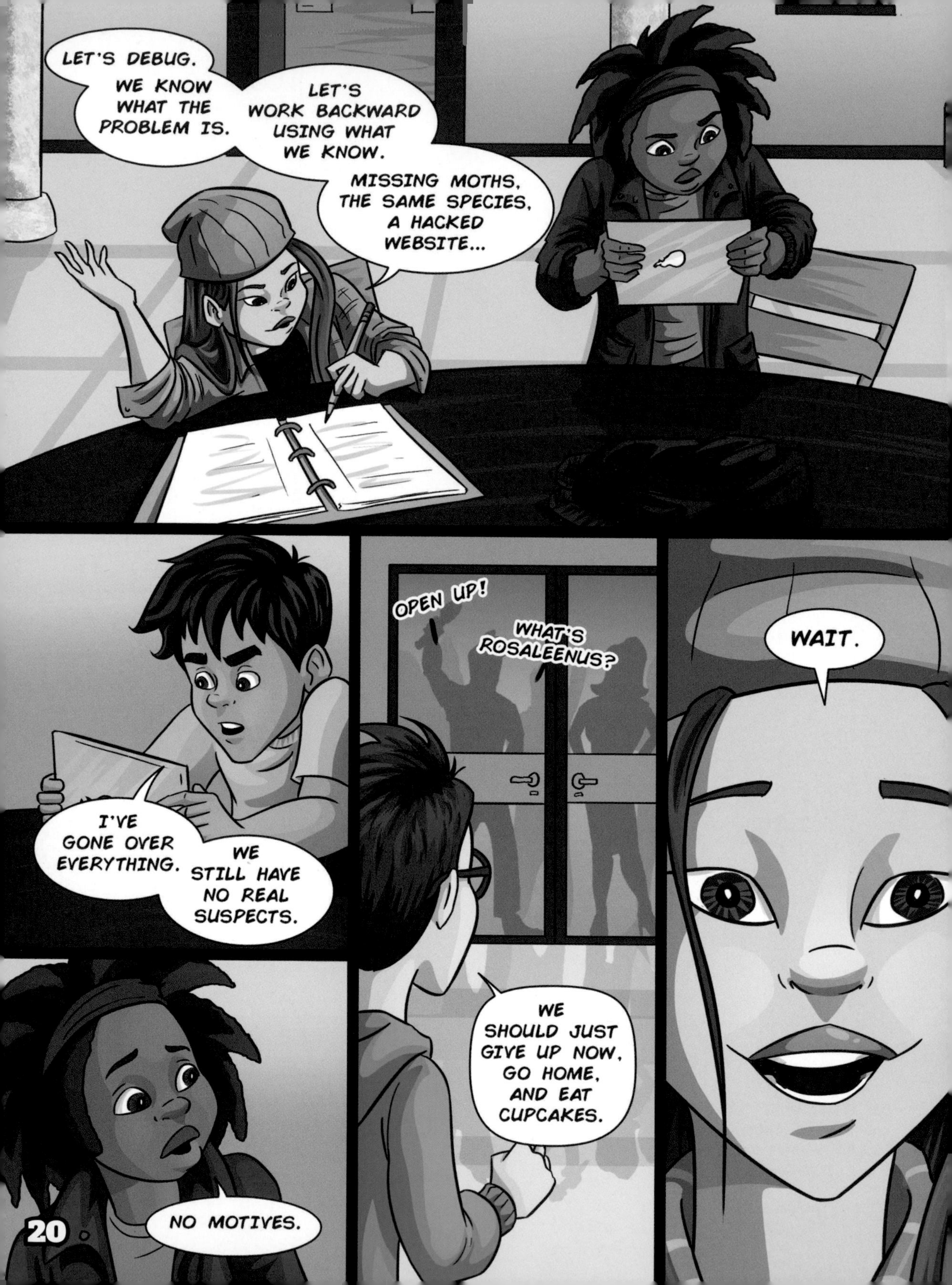
LET'S DEBUG.
WE KNOW WHAT THE PROBLEM IS.
LET'S WORK BACKWARD USING WHAT WE KNOW.
MISSING MOTHS, THE SAME SPECIES, A HACKED WEBSITE...
I'VE GONE OVER EVERYTHING.
WE STILL HAVE NO REAL SUSPECTS.
NO MOTIVES.
OPEN UP!
WHAT'S ROSALEENUS?
WE SHOULD JUST GIVE UP NOW, GO HOME, AND EAT CUPCAKES.
WAIT.

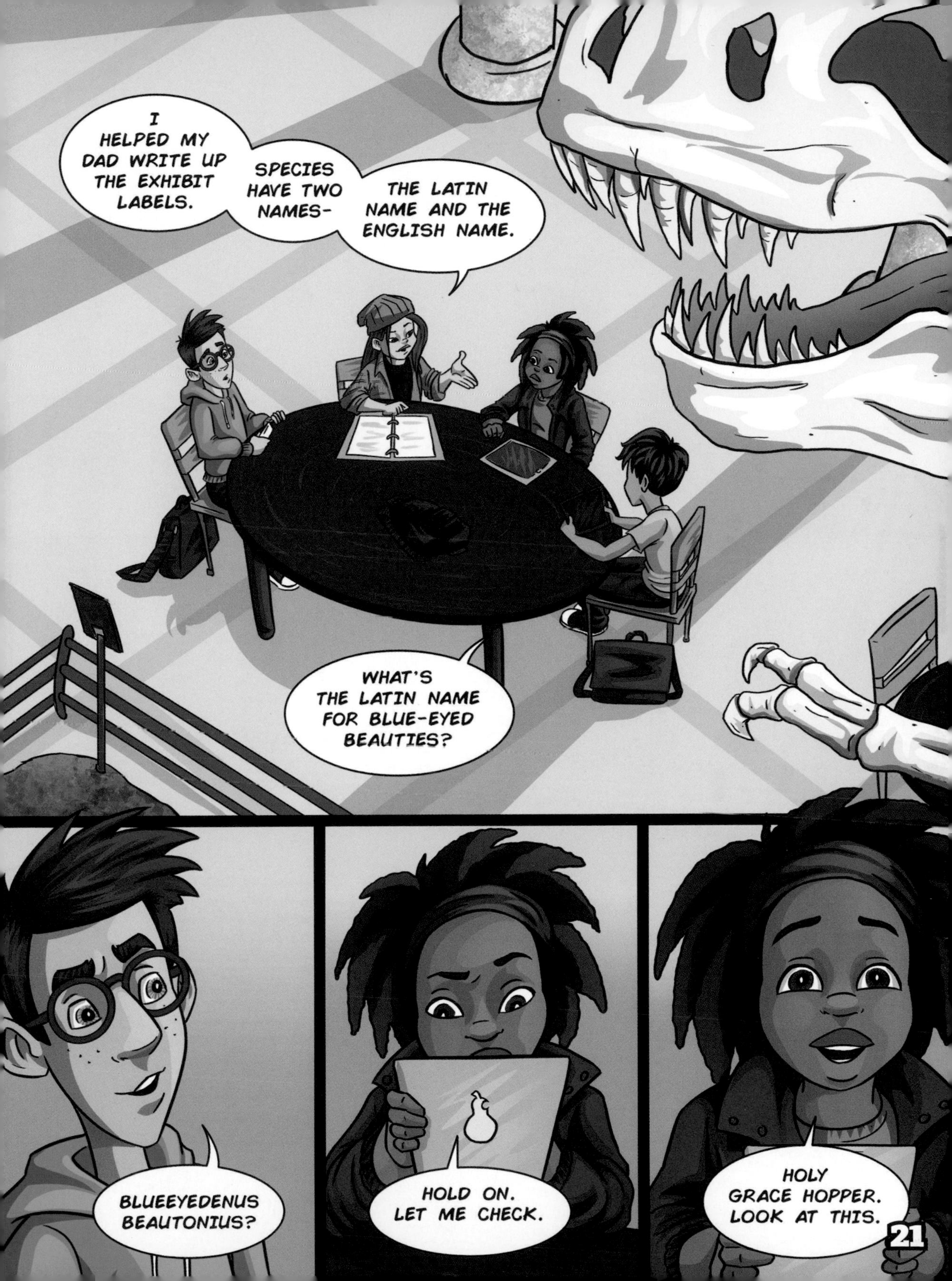
I HELPED MY DAD WRITE UP THE EXHIBIT LABELS.
SPECIES HAVE TWO NAMES-
THE LATIN NAME AND THE ENGLISH NAME.
WHAT'S THE LATIN NAME FOR BLUE-EYED BEAUTIES?
BLUEEYEDENUS BEAUTONIUS?
HOLD ON. LET ME CHECK.
HOLY GRACE HOPPER. LOOK AT THIS.

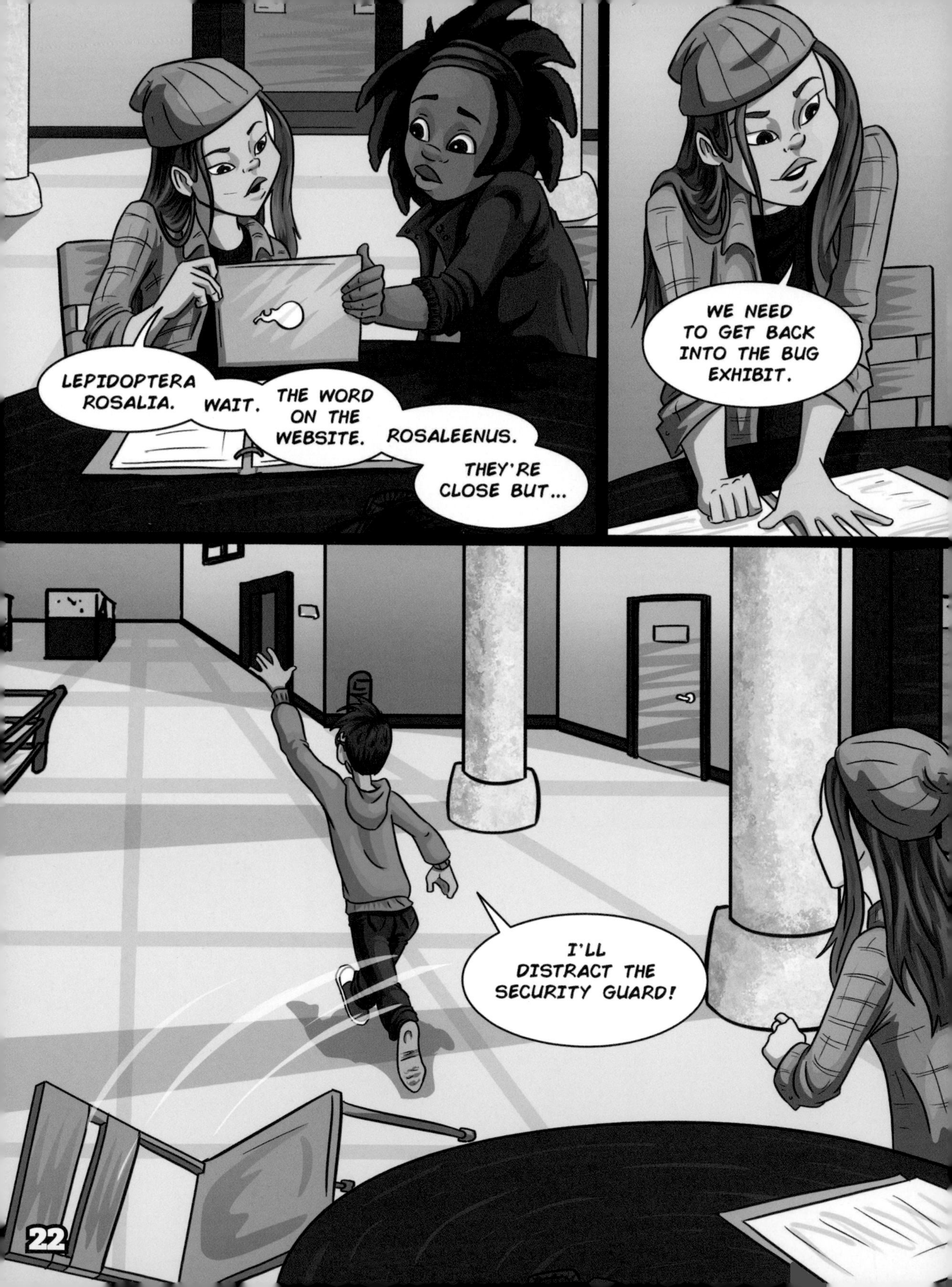
LEPIDOPTERA ROSALIA.
WAIT.
THE WORD ON THE WEBSITE.
ROSALEENUS.
THEY'RE CLOSE BUT...
WE NEED TO GET BACK INTO THE BUG EXHIBIT.
I'LL DISTRACT THE SECURITY GUARD!

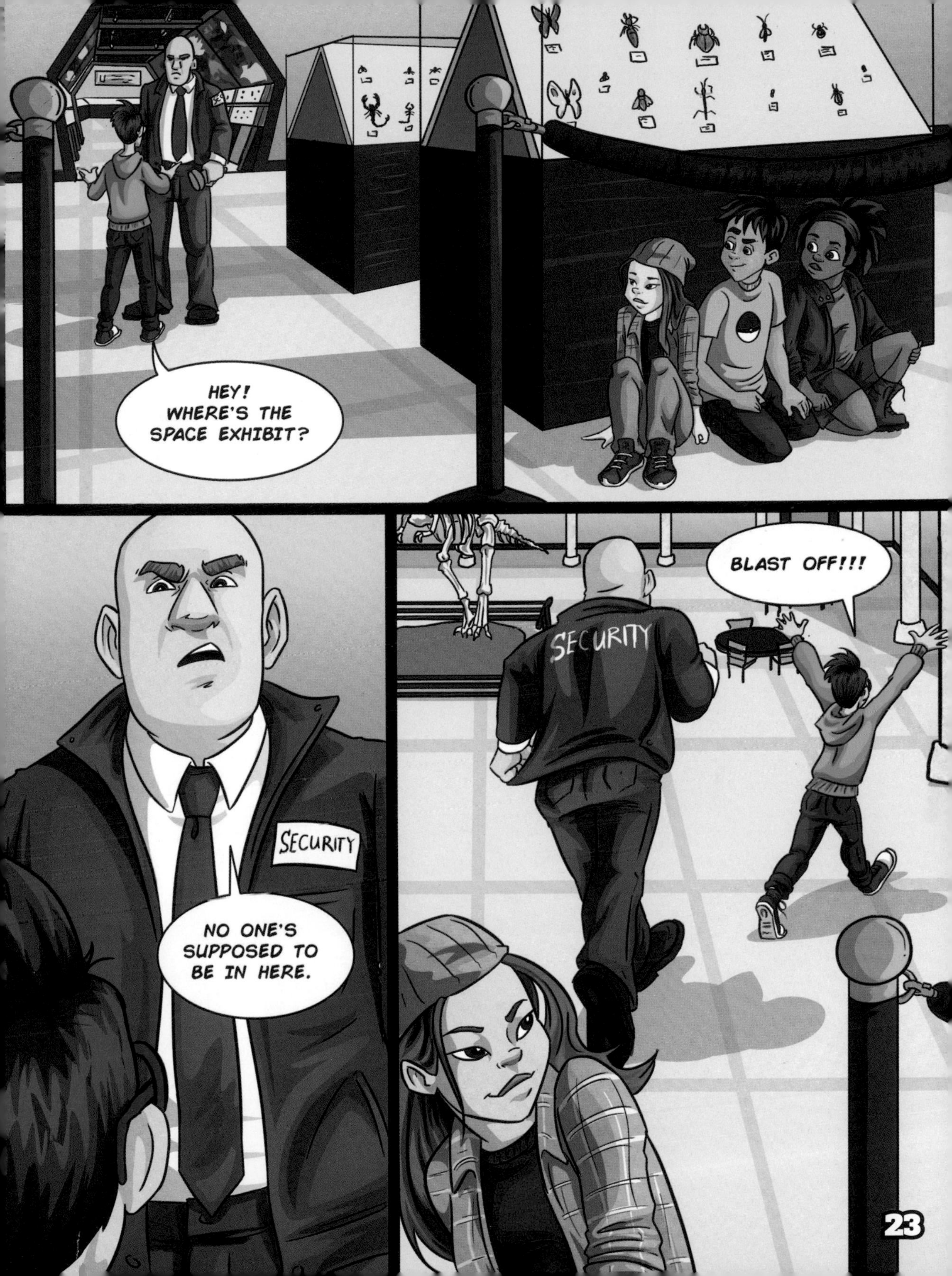
HEY! WHERE'S THE SPACE EXHIBIT?
NO ONE'S SUPPOSED TO BE IN HERE.
BLAST OFF!!!
SECURITY
SECURITY

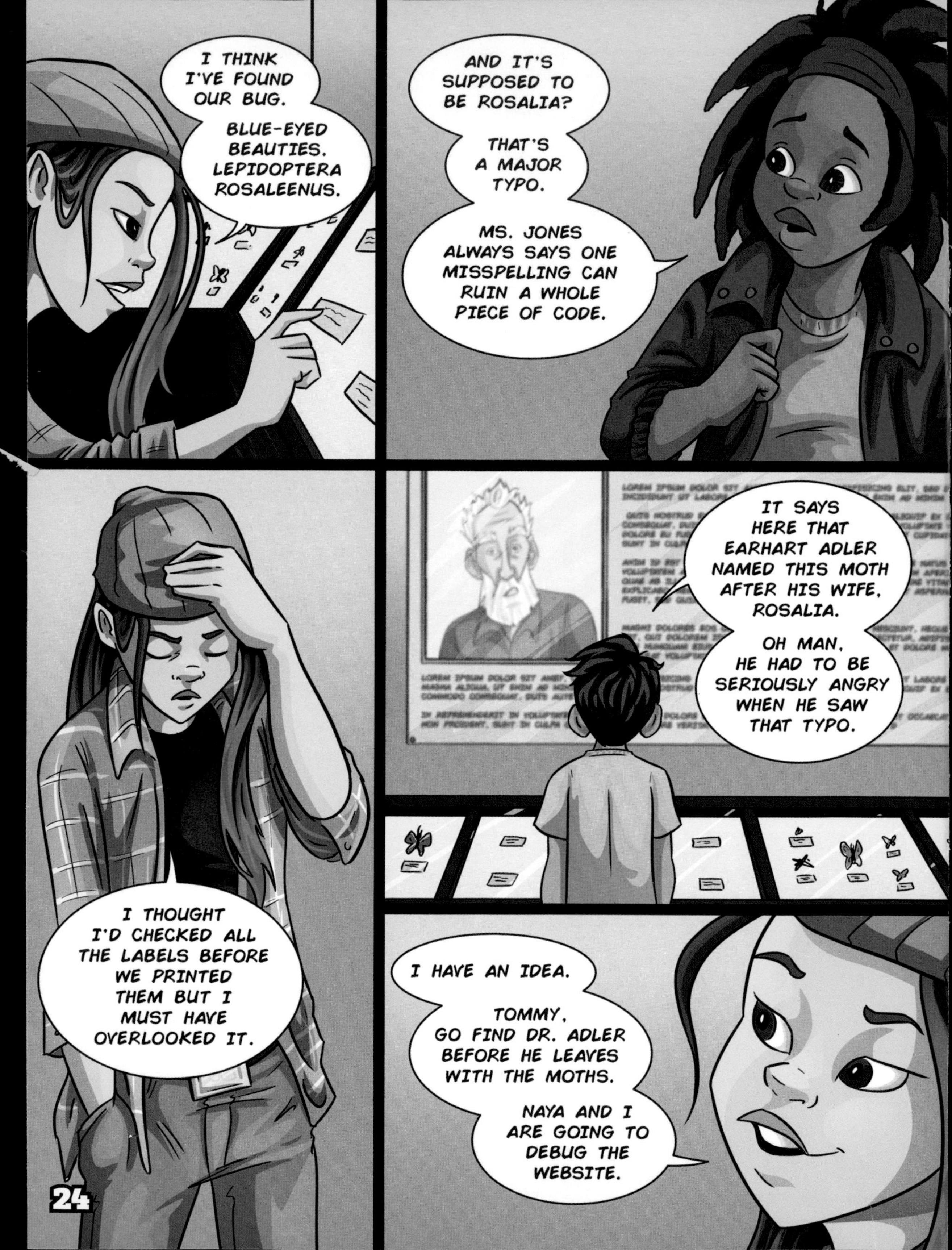
I THINK I'VE FOUND OUR BUG.
BLUE-EYED BEAUTIES. LEPIDOPTERA ROSALEENUS.
AND IT'S SUPPOSED TO BE ROSALIA?
THAT'S A MAJOR TYPO.
MS. JONES ALWAYS SAYS ONE MISSPELLING CAN RUIN A WHOLE PIECE OF CODE.
I THOUGHT I'D CHECKED ALL THE LABELS BEFORE WE PRINTED THEM BUT I MUST HAVE OVERLOOKED IT.
IT SAYS HERE THAT EARHART ADLER NAMED THIS MOTH AFTER HIS WIFE, ROSALIA.
OH MAN, HE HAD TO BE SERIOUSLY ANGRY WHEN HE SAW THAT TYPO.
I HAVE AN IDEA.
TOMMY, GO FIND DR. ADLER BEFORE HE LEAVES WITH THE MOTHS.
NAYA AND I ARE GOING TO DEBUG THE WEBSITE.

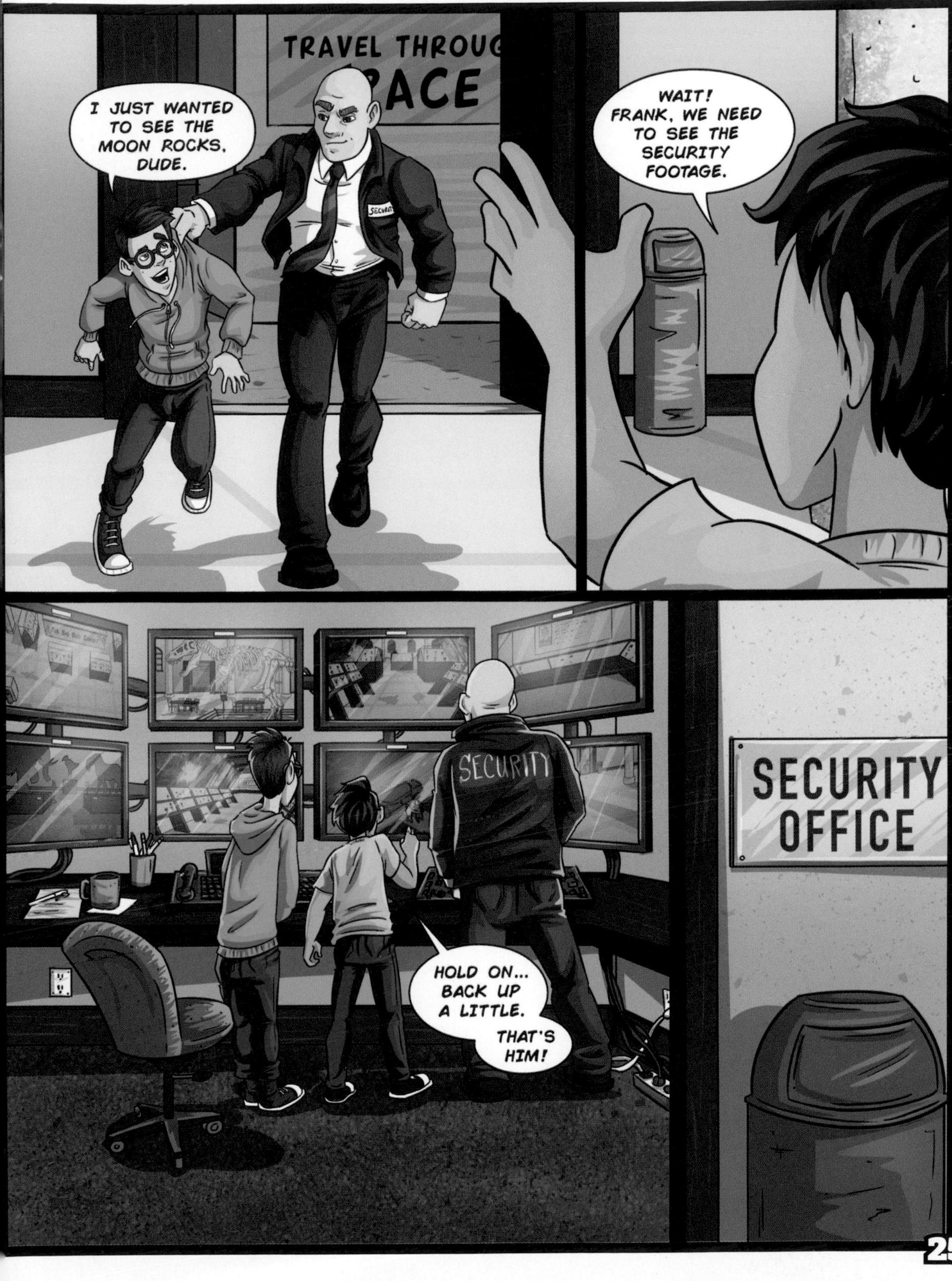
TRAVEL THROUG
ACE
I JUST WANTED TO SEE THE MOON ROCKS, DUDE.
WAIT! FRANK, WE NEED TO SEE THE SECURITY FOOTAGE.
SECURITY
HOLD ON... BACK UP A LITTLE.
THAT'S HIM!
SECURITY OFFICE

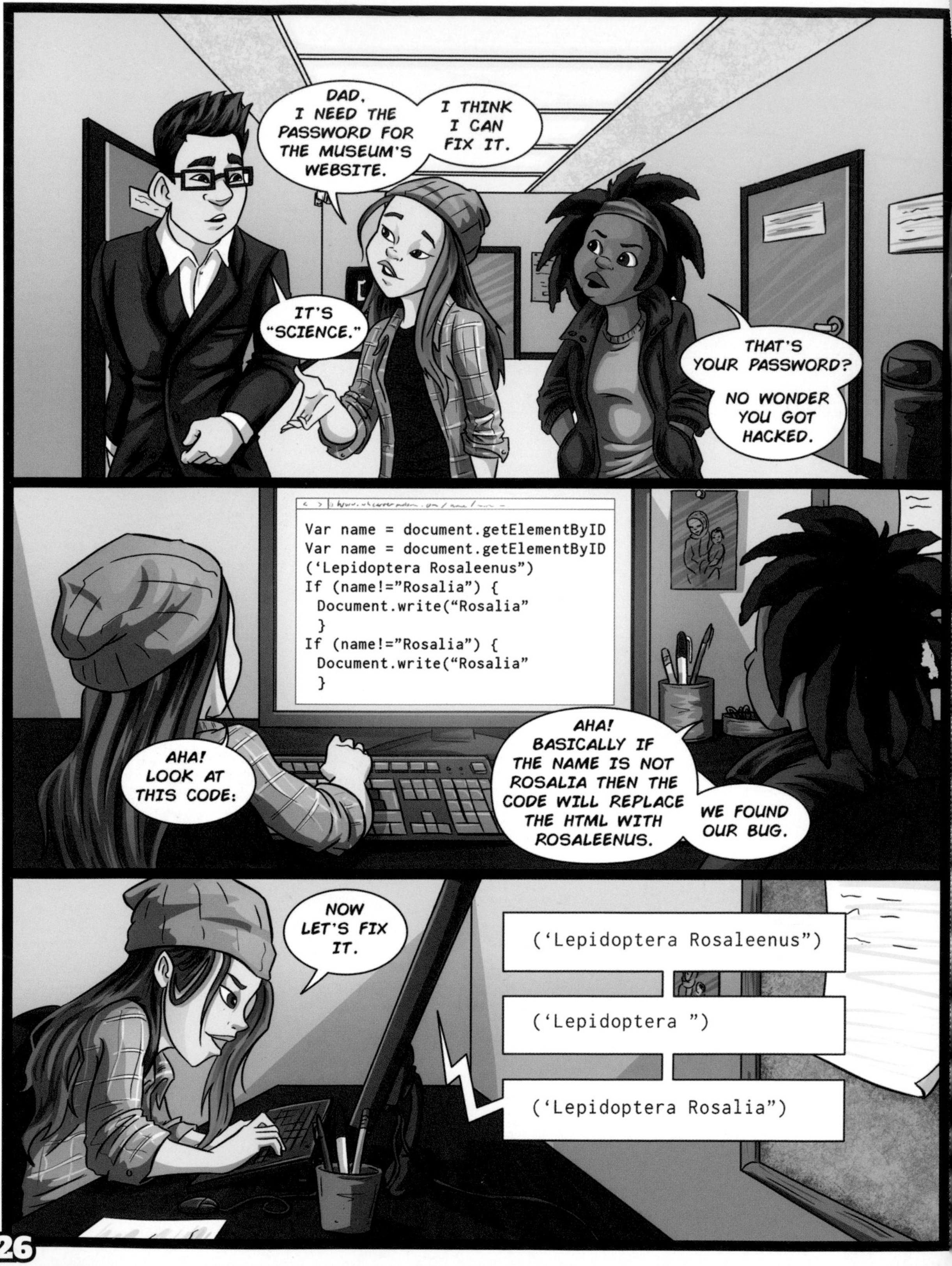

DAD, I NEED THE PASSWORD FOR THE MUSEUM'S WEBSITE.
I THINK I CAN FIX IT.
IT'S "SCIENCE."
THAT'S YOUR PASSWORD?
NO WONDER YOU GOT HACKED.
Var name = document.getElementByID
Var name = document.getElementByID
('Lepidoptera Rosaleenus")
If (name!="Rosalia") {
Document.write("Rosalia"
}
If (name!="Rosalia") {
Document.write("Rosalia"
}
AHA! LOOK AT THIS CODE:
AHA! BASICALLY IF THE NAME IS NOT ROSALIA THEN THE CODE WILL REPLACE THE HTML WITH ROSALEENUS.
WE FOUND OUR BUG.
NOW LET'S FIX IT.
('Lepidoptera Rosaleenus")
('Lepidoptera ")
('Lepidoptera Rosalia")

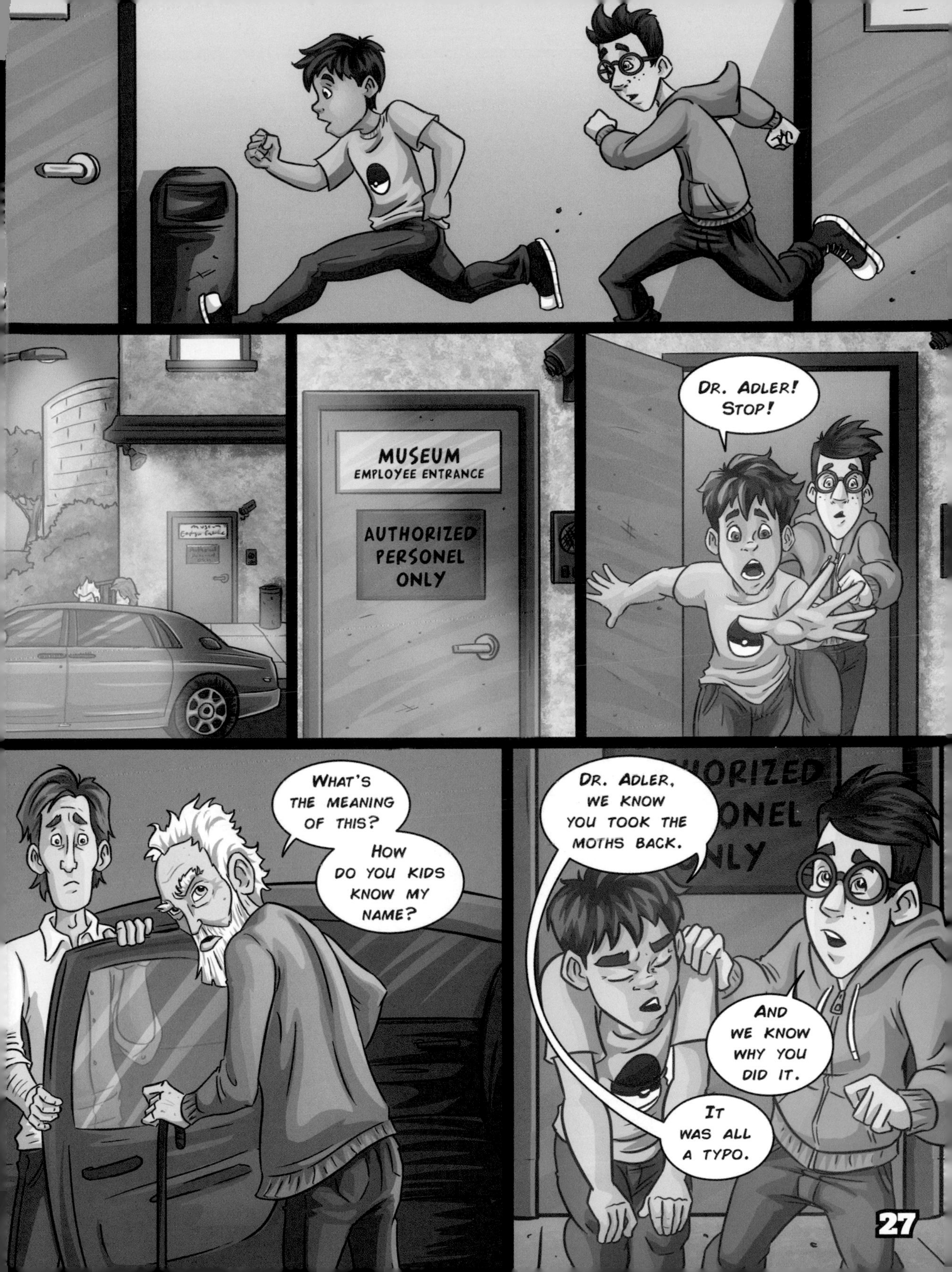
MUSEUM
EMPLOYEE ENTRANCE
AUTHORIZED PERSONEL ONLY
DR. ADLER! STOP!
WHAT'S THE MEANING OF THIS?
HOW DO YOU KIDS KNOW MY NAME?
DR. ADLER, WE KNOW YOU TOOK THE MOTHS BACK.
AND WE KNOW WHY YOU DID IT.
IT WAS ALL A TYPO.

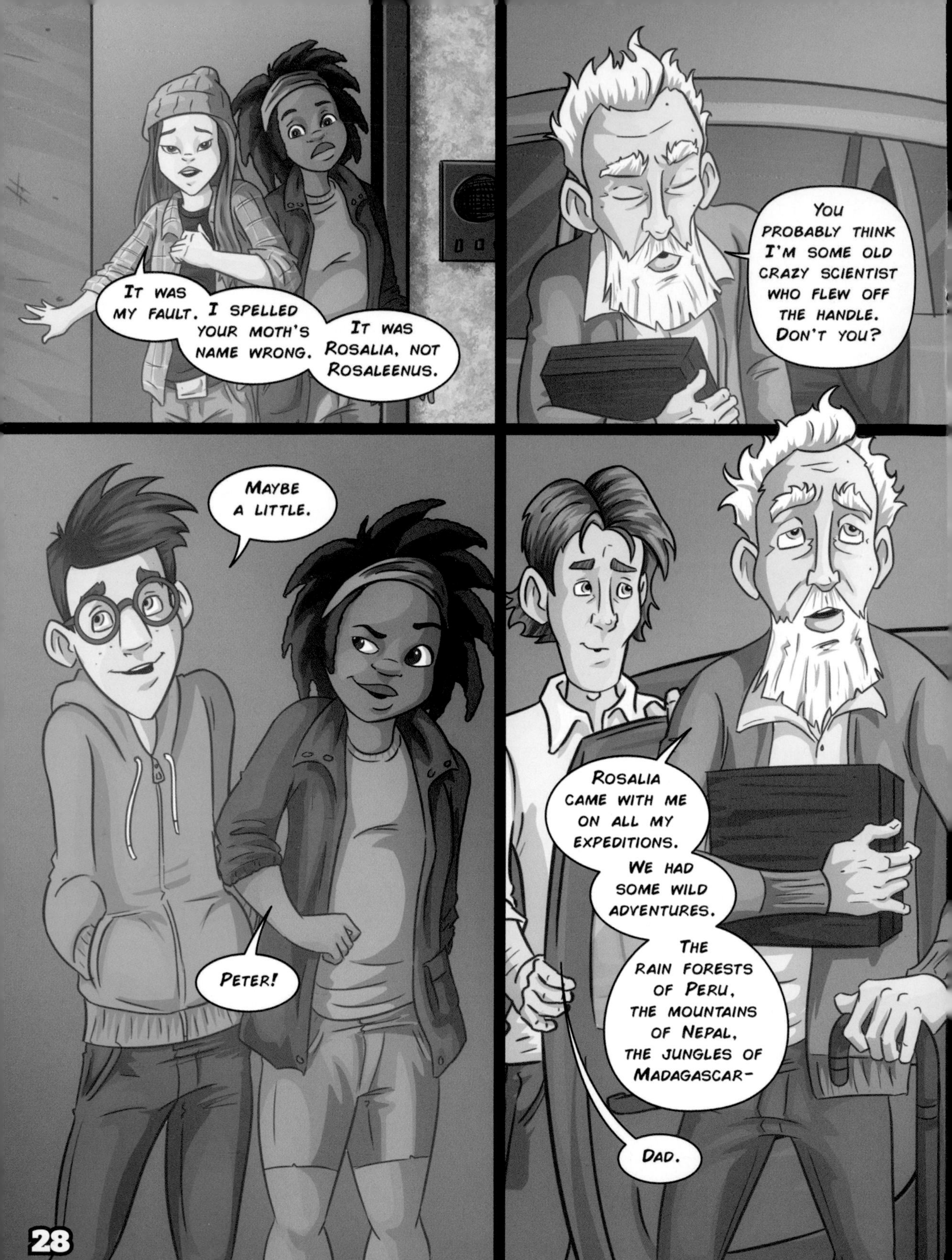
It was my fault. I spelled your moth's name wrong.
It was Rosalia, not Rosaleenus.
You probably think I'm some old crazy scientist who flew off the handle. Don't you?
Maybe a little.
Peter!
Rosalia came with me on all my expeditions.
We had some wild adventures.
The rain forests of Peru, the mountains of Nepal, the jungles of Madagascar-
Dad.

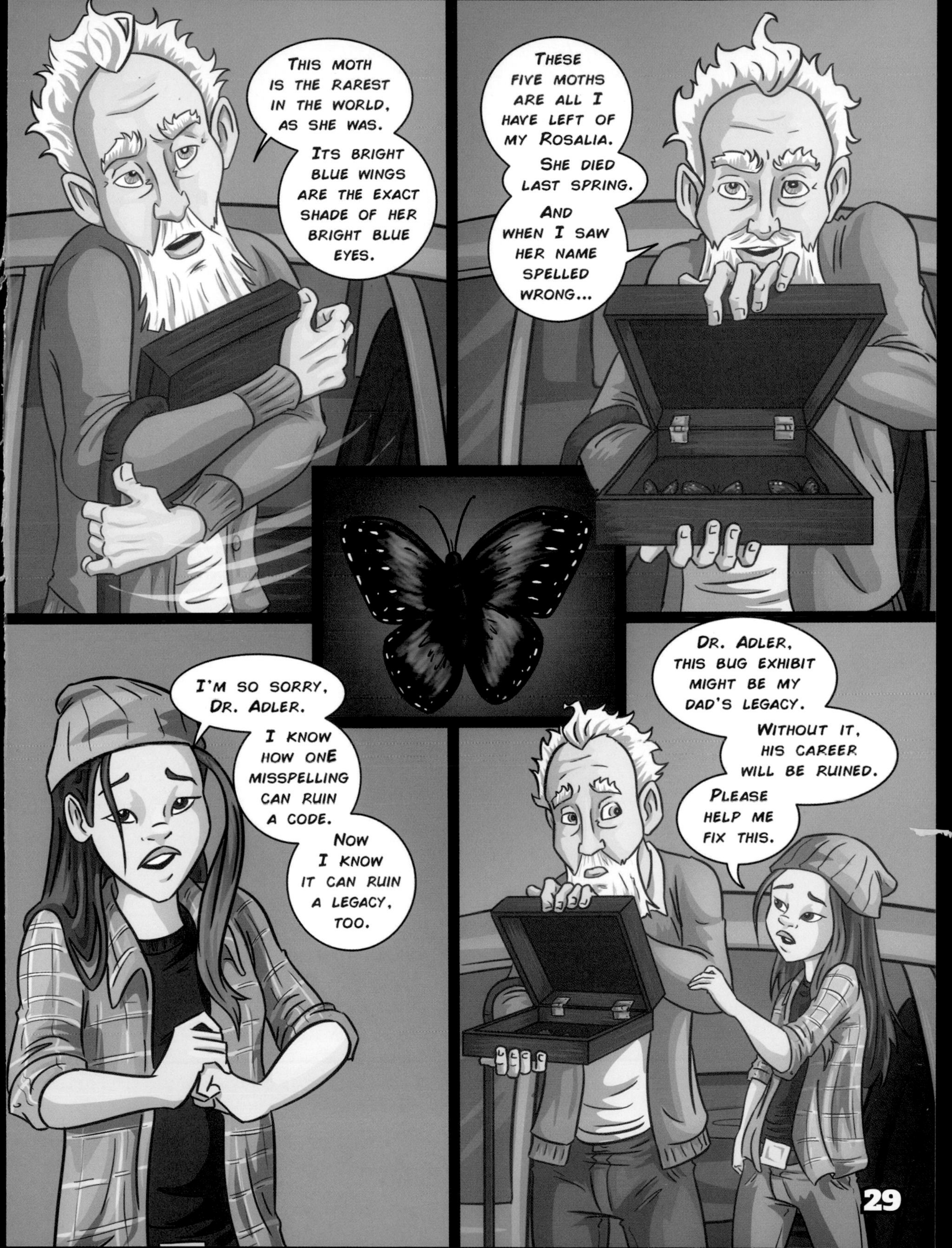
This moth is the rarest in the world, as she was.
Its bright blue wings are the exact shade of her bright blue eyes.
These five moths are all I have left of my Rosalia.
She died last spring.
And when I saw her name spelled wrong...
I'm so sorry, Dr. Adler.
I know how one misspelling can ruin a code.
Now I know it can ruin a legacy, too.
Dr. Adler, this bug exhibit might be my dad's legacy.
Without it, his career will be ruined.
Please help me fix this.

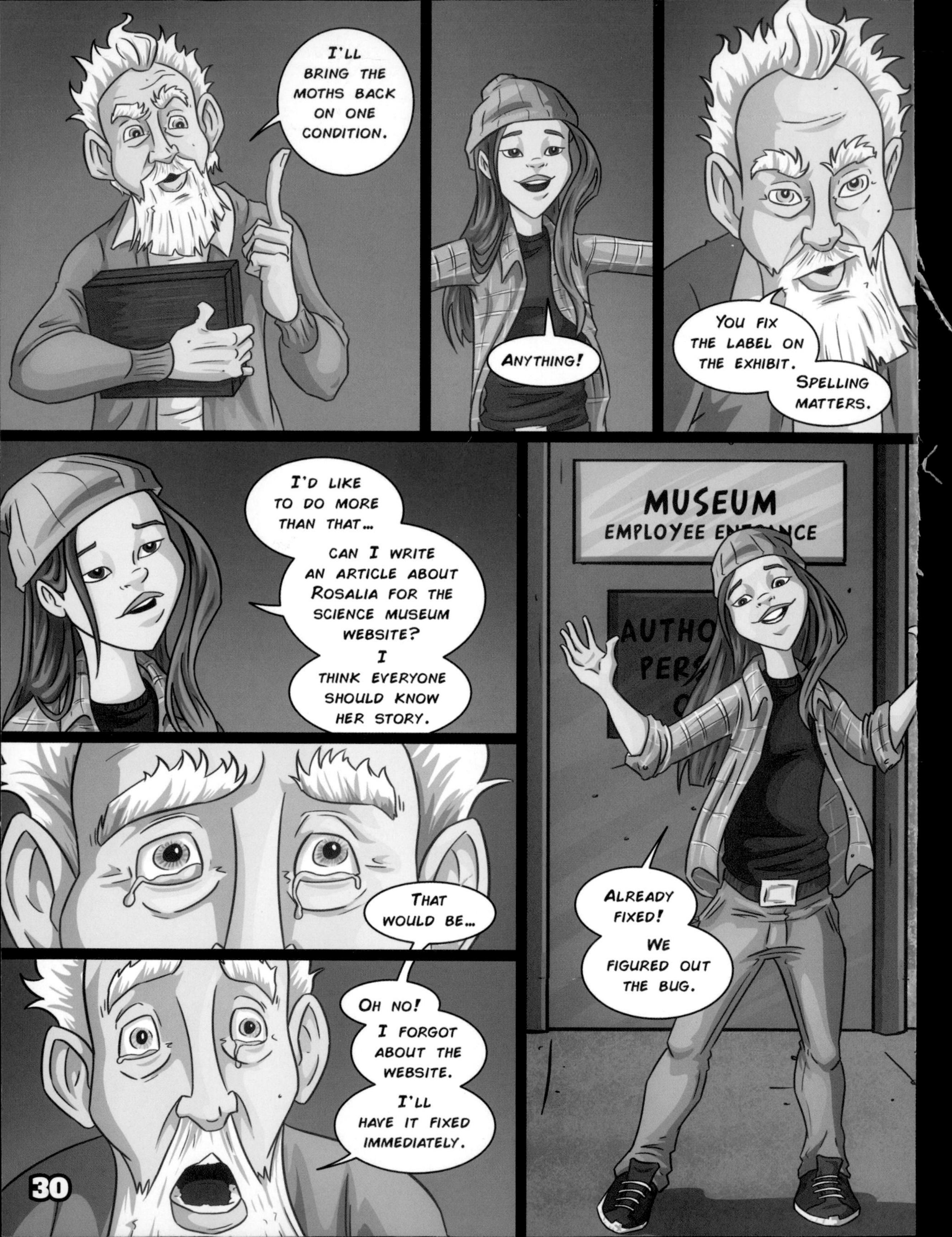
I'LL BRING THE MOTHS BACK ON ONE CONDITION.
ANYTHING!
YOU FIX THE LABEL ON THE EXHIBIT.
SPELLING MATTERS.
I'D LIKE TO DO MORE THAN THAT...
CAN I WRITE AN ARTICLE ABOUT ROSALIA FOR THE SCIENCE MUSEUM WEBSITE?
I THINK EVERYONE SHOULD KNOW HER STORY.
THAT WOULD BE...
OH NO!
I FORGOT ABOUT THE WEBSITE.
I'LL HAVE IT FIXED IMMEDIATELY.
MUSEUM
EMPLOYEE EN
CE
ALREADY FIXED!
WE FIGURED OUT THE BUG.

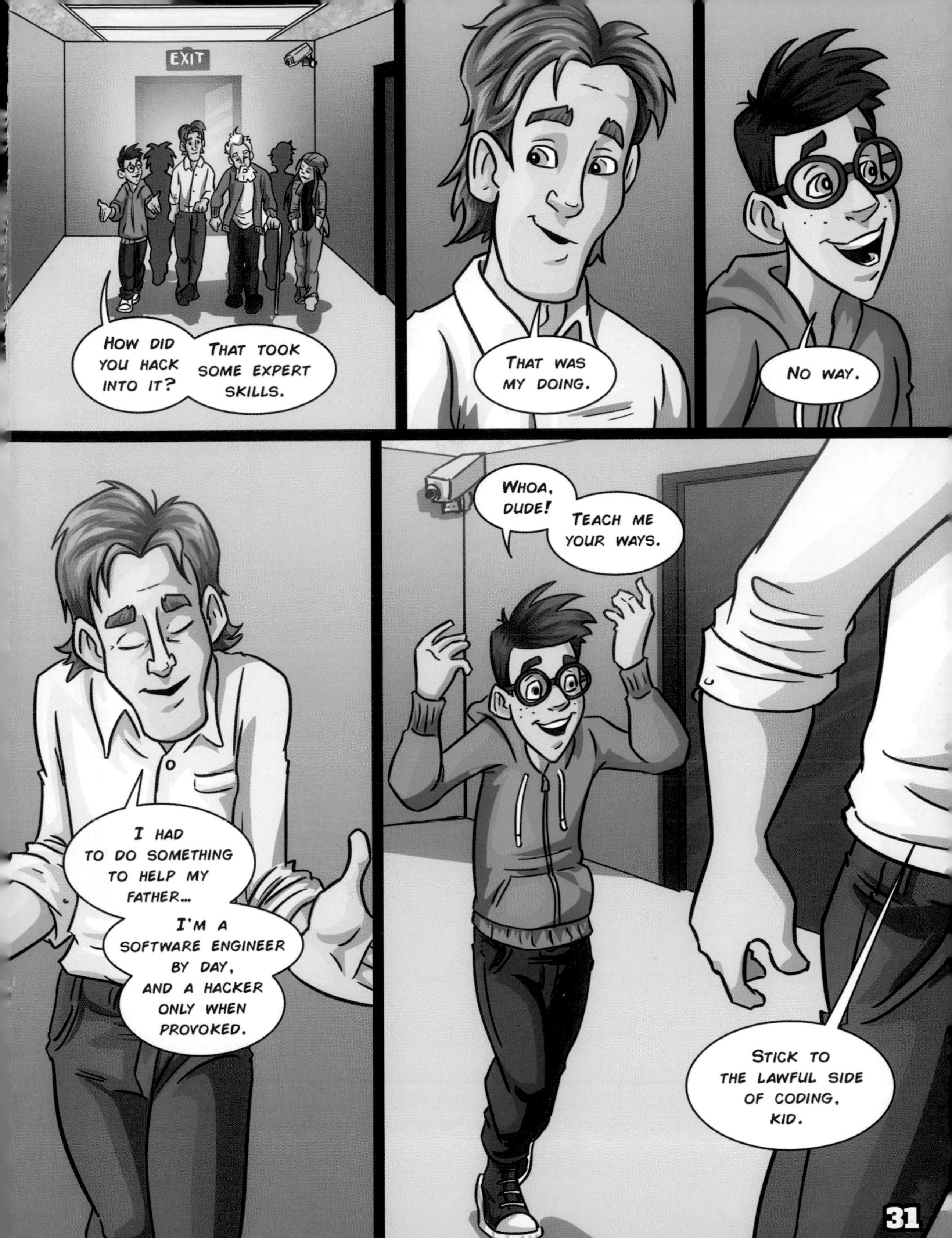
EXIT
HOW DID YOU HACK INTO IT?
THAT TOOK SOME EXPERT SKILLS.
THAT WAS MY DOING.
NO WAY.
I HAD TO DO SOMETHING TO HELP MY FATHER...
I'M A SOFTWARE ENGINEER BY DAY, AND A HACKER ONLY WHEN PROVOKED.
WHOA, DUDE!
TEACH ME YOUR WAYS.
STICK TO THE LAWFUL SIDE OF CODING, KID.

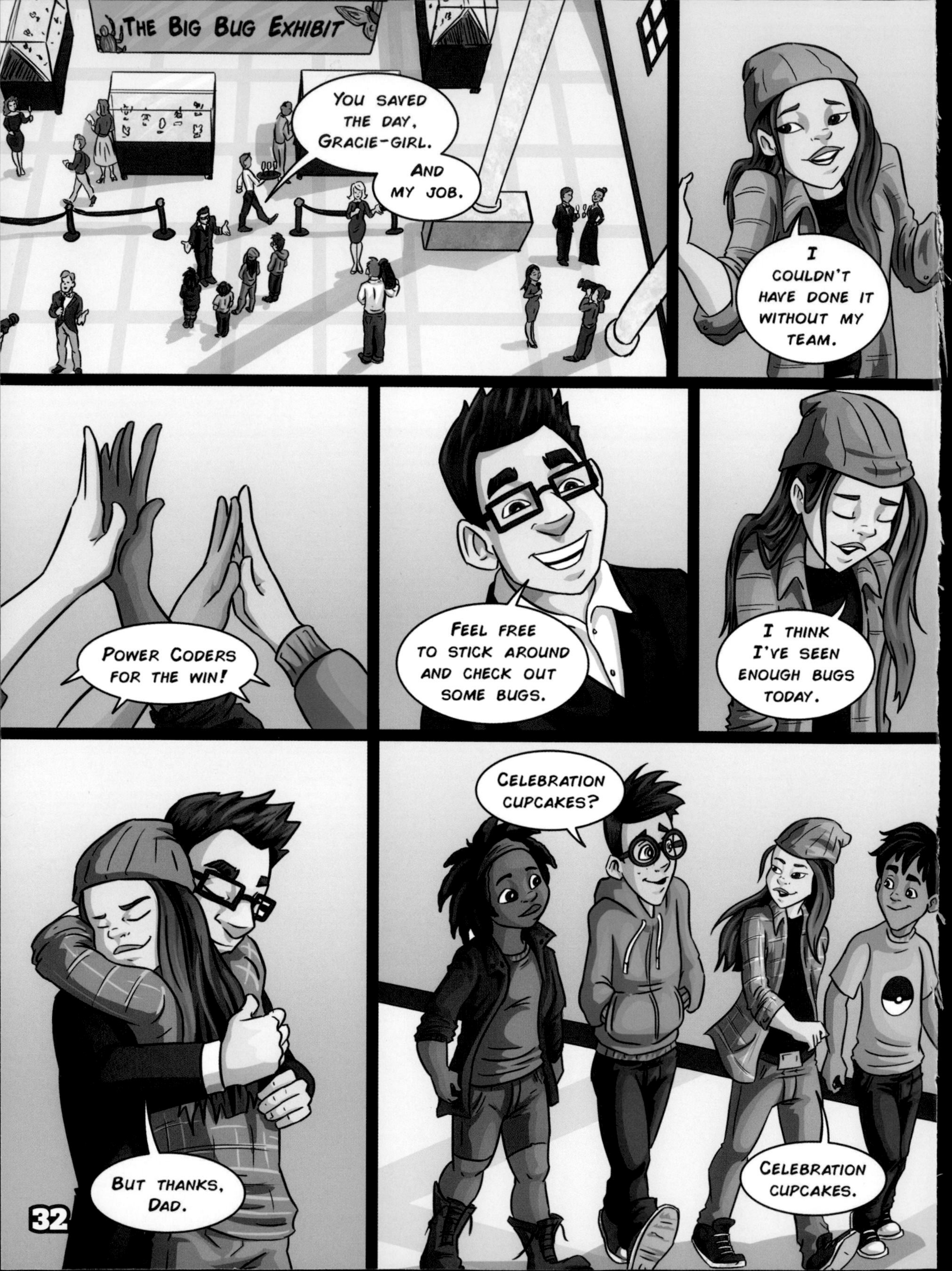
The Big Bug Exhibit
You saved the day, Gracie-girl.
And my job.
I couldn't have done it without my team.
Power Coders for the win!
Feel free to stick around and check out some bugs.
I think I've seen enough bugs today.
But thanks, Dad.
Celebration cupcakes?
Celebration cupcakes.

3/19